D0365092

The Urbana Free Library

To renew materials call
217-367-4057

The Annex

The Annex

Russell James

Five Star • Waterville, Maine

Five Star First Edition Mystery Series.

Published in 2002 in conjunction with
Tekno Books and Ed Gorman.

Set in 11 pt. Plantin by Elena Picard.

Printed in the United States on permanent paper.

Library of Congress Cataloging-in-Publication Data

James, Russell.
    The annex / Russell James.
        p. cm.—(Five Star first edition mystery series)
    ISBN 0-7862-3931-X (hc : alk. paper)
    1. Triangles (Interpersonal relations)—Fiction.
    2. Architects—Fiction. 3. Chauffeurs—Fiction.
    4. Extortion—Fiction. 5. England—Fiction.
    I. Title. II. Series.
    PR6060.A473 A84 2002
    823′.914—dc21   2001058555

The Annex

Act One

Alsemero:

'Twas in the temple where I first beheld her,
And now again the same: what omen yet
Follows of that? none but imaginary;
Why should my hopes or fate be timorous?

The Changeling,
by Thomas Middleton & William Rowley

Act One, Scene One.

Chapter 1

Joanna looked down from her window. Soapy water glistened on his hard flesh, his muscles glinted in the sun, and water streaked down his blue jeans. On Florian's wet skin, lazy blobs of foam slid like melting ice cream. A spurting hose jerked in his hands and he held it loosely, pointing at the car, splashing the jet carelessly across the shining metal of Miro's red Ferrari. Miro's Ferrari. Miro's car. Miro's house, garden, hosepipe. The man down there, playing with Miro's car, was Miro's. She was Miro's. The whole place . . .

She looked across the cobbled drive, beyond the gardens and lush lawn, to the boundary wall, newly built in Cotswold stone. The double gates in sinuous wrought iron stood higher than the walls. The gates were newly built as well. In the morning sun the brass finials looked vulgar, she thought, slightly too bright. Surprising for Miro, who normally had perfect taste.

Perhaps he didn't want his house too perfect. She had read somewhere that when a Muslim made a carpet—one of those magical Eastern carpets—he always left a tiny flaw, to show God he had not presumed too far. Only God could achieve perfection. Miro's flaw was that set of knobs.

Or perhaps it was the annex.

She glanced back at Florian, washing the car. He was *far* from perfect. Beads of water sparkled on his hair. His face

9

glistened. His body was damp, sticky with sweat. She saw him spray the jet straight up in the air, so that for a brief moment it formed a sparkling umbrella of rain beneath which he stood, face uplifted, eyes tightly shut as spray fell down.

Joanna stepped back from the window. He mustn't see her watching. These last two weeks Florian had been watching her. For these last two weeks, when she had practically moved in with Miro, when everyone knew she'd soon be Mrs. Vermont, Miro's driver had stared at her. Perhaps he thought his ugliness allowed him to—but she loathed him.

Joanna glanced towards the bathroom door. Miro was out of sight but shaving, humming to himself in the way he always did, pulling his razor carefully through the lather as if it were an artist's palette knife, carving a channel through the expensive foam and leaving a faint stubble on his pink, clean skin. He was a hairy man, shaved twice a day, while the menial Florian who thought so much of himself hardly needed to shave at all.

Jo edged back to the curtain and peeped down again. Yes, naked to the waist, shameless, not a hair to see on him. Chest as smooth as plastic. It could have been *made* of plastic; his torso looked pre-moulded, every muscle in place and not a scrap of flab. It was—in a way that didn't interest her at all—a textbook body. It could have been photographed as a guide to male anatomy. Every piece correctly sized. Muscles rippling beneath the skin. Not overdeveloped muscles—he wasn't one of those men who practised with weights each day in front of a ballerina's mirror. As far as she knew, Florian didn't use weights at all. Though he did go running. She had seen him once, loose in his track suit, jogging up the drive after a run across the fields. Another annoying thing about him: after his run he had looked less sweaty than he did now, washing the car—so perhaps he wasn't sweating down there beneath the window; perhaps that silver sheen was water; perhaps he liked the feel of water on his skin.

It was so hot today. Barely nine o'clock and already the sun was above the trees and bleaching the sky. June. A British heat wave. She'd have to stay indoors today, keep to the shadows. Despite her olive colouring she avoided sun. An hour out there and she would frazzle. Just the thought could make her itch. When she was a kid she would break out in heat rashes and her mother had bought her a soppy, wide-brimmed hat. But she wouldn't wear it. People laughed at her, she said. She learned to dress coolly and sit in the shade.

Jo turned away. In the bathroom she heard Miro pull the plug. She waited while he filled a glass. She smiled: time for the morning tooth scrubbing ritual. But at Miro's age he was entitled to have regular habits—he had life in control. He was forty-two and knew how the world worked. He was confident in it. Miro's confidence was Joanna's strength. She was inexperienced—not yet twenty-one and, before she met Miro, lightly travelled, untutored and barely able to read a menu. But he was steering her effortlessly through the complex mysteries of a finer, adult world—good restaurants, music, theatre, ballet. He had bought her clothes and taught her how to think. No doubt people whispered that he was a father figure and yes, perhaps he was, but he was an ideal father, one who sheltered his daughter and expressed a father's love. She loved him for it. He opened the world for her.

She heard him scrubbing vigorously. She knew he was still humming to himself because it sounded as if he were gargling in there. Water splashed into the sink.

Down on the cobbles Florian was playing with the hose-pipe, dangling it from his hands and squirting water on what remained of the lather. He placed a bare foot on the rubber hose to make the stream spurt in starts at the gleaming car. A

11

bare foot—yes, the disgusting man was standing on damp cobbles barefoot, wearing nothing but jeans, probably not even underpants, and the wasteful water streamed off the surface of the shining red car, puddled on the cobbles and glistened all over his lithe body, to make his muscles shine. His hair was wetter now. Water clung to it like pearls. Looking down at him, she could see how hot the sun was. From a hundred small puddles arose a slight haze of shimmering vapour. Florian shook his head, scattering flecks of water and laughing in the sun. But he hadn't seen her. He didn't look up. He was lost in some strange world of his own. Fantasising. Pretending he owned the car. Being a kid again with the powerful hose. Suddenly he sprayed it, making a long arc that reached right over the car towards the flower bed. He was playing now. He wasn't washing the car. This was too much: she must tell Miro.

Before moving back inside the bedroom she took a final glance at Florian. He was streaming wet now. Then he turned round—and when he did he showed the other side of his face—the side that showed his scarred, repulsive cheek. She could see his ugliness now, his birthmark. That puckered skin was an insult to anyone who looked. Of course one should feel sorry for him—but she didn't: that was what he wanted.

Miro appeared from the bathroom.

"Waiting?" he asked, a huge towel around his waist.

"You're worth waiting for."

He threw his arms wide and looked down at his hairy white body. "Not bad for a man of thirty-eight."

"Forty-two."

"You know too much, young lady."

He grinned and strode to the bed for his clothes. For a man over forty, she thought, his body was by no means bad. He might be carrying a few extra pounds, but that was inevitable, surely? He wasn't fat, he was . . . chunky. He certainly didn't lack strength in bed. Miro could be summed up by his wiry hair—black with grey streaks, strong, upright and just a hint unruly. He had steel blue eyes. There were times he stared at her when she felt pierced to the core.

If they had come in the Lexus it would have created no great impression, but the red Ferrari turned everyone's head. Miro wanted to make an entrance, and when he and Jo arrived in the gleaming drop-head sports car, you could hear builders' hammers drop to the ground. Miro drove himself, of course. Not that he wouldn't trust Florian with the car, but to let someone drive him here would create the wrong image. Miro was able to buy the car and drive it.

He swept across the huge, empty, white-lined car park and stopped at an angle by the glass doors. Leaping out athletically, he nipped around the car and opened the other door for Joanna, who waited inside as he had told her. Knowing that the eyes of the waiting party would be upon her she stepped out carefully, one long leg stretched like a proboscis to scent the new-laid tarmac, then the other leg laid slowly by it, both knees bent, the short skirt rumpled up along her thigh as she took her weight on thin high heels, her hand extended to Miro so he could help her from the car. The seat was low and she needed a helping hand—just as Miro needed the buzz of helping his woman from his car: his elegant, gorgeous, olive skinned, immaculately dressed, long legged, young, untouchable appendage. His prize in the game of life.

No one would have known that she was nervous. No one would have known that she struggled with her role: twenty years old, the centre of attention, like a visiting film star. But she was just a local girl. Here at the site, any one of those labourers might have gone to school with her. What if one called out, "Hey Jo, remember me? Are you too good for your old friends now?"

From the small group at the glass doorway, a man stepped forward. The three beside him twitched, as if they wanted to come as well. They kept their eyes on Joanna. On the red tiled roof, two workmen looked down. In a suspended cradle, a window cleaner watched. Another man leant on his broom. Behind the glass wall of the almost-ready supermarket, three shopfitters drifted closer so they could see.

The top man had arrived.

Miro Vermont was senior partner and head architect in the firm of consulting engineers responsible for the site—not just the main building, the supermarket, but the whole estate: the concession stores, the filling station, the car park, even the raised flower beds in stark white concrete bays. Despite the dominating presence of the supermarket, the retail park had been designed to resemble an idealised market square: brick fascias, red tiles, a stand-alone ice cream bar, tender young trees. Each of the concessions had been made deliberately different, so that rather than blend in to the overall scheme they stood out as real shops in a real market square—though half of them were owned by the supermarket company. It owned the ice cream stall as well, but had sacrificed sixteen parking spaces beside the stall to accommodate an island of Astroturf like a village green. Presentation was Miro's skill—like his entrance, with the red Ferrari and his girl.

He led Jo inside—the glass doors opening automatically, as they soon would a million times a year for shoppers with wire trolleys—and the doors quivered slightly as they marked the respectful gap left between the presidential couple and their watchful retinue, several paces behind. The store was fully aisled but as yet unstocked and in this waiting state looked twice its size.

The man who had greeted them began babbling about the high standard of finish, the timetable, the excellence of the glass frontage, but Jo wasn't listening. She doubted Miro was either. His work was done. He strode through the aisles, looking for faults. It was absolutely vital, he had told Jo, that he found things he could complain of, that his sharp eyes were never satisfied, that the on-site team were kept on their toes.

"Two days," he announced as if they didn't know. "Before the client starts stocking up. So come what may, we finish to-morrow. Right lads, we've seen what the public sees, so let's have a look out back."

Once they had stepped beyond the service doors the high finish stopped. Here, the offices, corridors and storage areas were plain and basic. Money had been saved. Painted walls, hard floors, unshielded lighting. Miro regretted the need to skimp in these back areas. The cramped offices were not conducive to creative thinking, he thought, but perhaps the retail management didn't want that from their staff.

The site manager, Rowley, was showing him everything, even the staff lavatories, during which Miro tried to remain sharp and vigilant. Joanna, he noticed, had glazed over. Out in the main store was a world she knew, but the back was drab and smelt of penny pinching. She had switched off now.

As he and Rowley passed from the undecorated corridors out to the high-roofed Goods Inwards bay, Rowley had the sense to speak first. "We have a slight problem."

"Bit late for that." Miro was glancing quickly round the bay, trying to see the problem before Rowley pointed it out.

"Goods Inwards door. It runs fine, but it's not high enough."

"Not high enough?"

At the touch of a switch the gleaming metal door would

15

roll up to the ceiling to expose the cavernous opening.

Rowley said, "We had a lorry arrive. It couldn't get through." He grimaced. "It's tall enough for their lorries but some suppliers use non-standard containers. They're the problem."

"How big a problem?"

"A few centimetres, that's all, but . . ."

"Can't we . . . ?" Miro shook his head irritably.

"The door's a solid unit."

"For Goodness sake," snapped Miro. "Can't they tell their suppliers to . . ."

"Use standard trucks? No, a supplier uses whatever he likes. Some come from the continent—"

Jo wandered off. Miro stayed with Rowley. "How the hell did you get us into this? The door height, for God's sake—it's elementary."

"We followed the plans." Rowley did not say *your* plans. He didn't need to.

"This is your site, Rowley. You're responsible."

Rowley stood patiently while Miro raged. When the noise subsided Rowley knew he would be in the clear. Miro must have already realised that this was a cock-up in his own office—understandable perhaps, but a cock-up nevertheless.

Miro sensed the man's growing confidence. He also saw that Jo was watching their exchange. "Look, Rowley, you're in charge here. When did this oversize container arrive?"

"Last evening."

"Yesterday?" Miro had him now. "Every hour counts, for God's sake. There's a fleet of trucks coming the day after next. And you have sat on this since yesterday? I'm disappointed, Rowley."

"I was waiting for—"

"Sort it. That's what I pay you for."

16

Chapter 2

Joanna wore her wedding dress. She fingered the white silk organza and the subtle embroidery across her breast. She had tried the dress on three times before and whenever she did so she felt disappointment. Plain white. So understated it looked ordinary. All the work was in the detail. On its hanger the dress seemed to droop slightly, to hide its light, and she felt that on the big day she might droop herself. But on her own wedding day she must be the star. Miro had been with her originally, had helped her choose this particular dress, had convinced her that this traditional Elizabethan style made her look magnificent. He wanted white, of course. Traditional. Virginal. He wasn't here with her today—hadn't seen her *in* the dress. She turned to Dee: "What do you *really* think?"

"Posh. Very Tatler."

That pleased the boutique owner: "You look wonderful."

Dee was as crisp as bridal lace. White blonde hair, sharp perky features; she wore a summer shift of red. Jo trusted her. They had been at school together. Being one of the few school friends Jo still had, Dee would be her bridesmaid.

Jo stood awkwardly, a gangly schoolgirl in her uniform. The manageress said, "Slip your shoes off. You'll be wearing flat satin pumps."

"I can't spend all day in flatties."

"They'll be just right for that dress—and much more

comfortable. It'll be a tiring day."

"I bet."

"The most wonderful day of your life."

"Oh, yeah."

"For Goodness sake," Dee laughed. "Make an effort! It looks fantastic. Kick your shoes off and stand up straight."

Jo stooped to remove a shoe. "Ouch," she muttered.

Dee said, "It'll look lovely with the headdress."

"There's a pin here somewhere. It scratched me."

The manageress dived in immediately, apologising as she found the pin. Jo said, "There isn't a bloodstain, is there? It'll ruin the dress."

But the manageress was holding the material away from Jo's skin. "No, no. I'm so sorry. Are you all right?"

"No more pins, are there?"

"Don't worry. No damage done."

Dee said, "I could kill for a dress like that."

They came out of the shop into a blast of sunshine. As they fixed their sunglasses, Dee said, "I hate to think what those dresses cost."

"Don't ask."

Florian had brought the Lexus right outside. As he opened the rear door Jo said, "We're going for coffee," and swept away.

He called, "When shall I come for you?"

Jo pretended not to hear, but Dee turned to Florian with a smile. "Can you collect us from Gino's—around twelve?"

Florian nodded. "It's a yellow line there, so look out for me."

He watched the pair of them flounce away.

Dee said, "We can sit outside. Then we'll see him when he arrives."

"It's his job to wait for us. That's what he's paid for."

"Oh, my." Dee nudged her playfully. "Who's getting used to fancy living?"

"No—"

"Ordering servants about."

Joanna blushed. "It's not that. He's creepy."

"Never carry on with servants. That's what I say."

"No chance."

"You know what you're like with boyfriends, Jo—the latest is always the greatest. No one else exists."

"Miro's different. He's more than a boyfriend."

"So don't go for his chauffeur. Take a shine to him, and then *Miro* won't exist."

"He's horrible. That face! If I had my way I'd sack the man, but Miro swears by him."

"Sack him! Wow. That's a bit extreme. You *have* moved up in the world, haven't you? I just hope you'll keep a place for me."

Dee eyed her sideways and Jo said, "You're my best friend. Whatever happens, there'll always be a place for you."

The blue river sparkled in bright sun. Its green banks were crammed with billowing marquees, smart cafe tables, canvas windbreaks and expensively dressed revellers braying in the light. Henley Royal Regatta blossoms each year at the end of June. For that week every scrap of river bank is blanketed with corporate hospitality booths, garden parties, trade stands and concession stalls. Jazz bands play in the open air. Streets throng. In rented hospitality enclaves, men in boaters and striped blazers outnumber women in summer frocks. They drink champagne and eat canapés. Intermittently they gossip and discuss business. They glance occasionally to-wards muscular young men whipping along the river in sleek

19

rowing boats. Before their disinterested gaze there passes an endless series of elimination rounds, with cups for this, chalices for that—all replayed on corporate TV monitors under corporate canvas. All ignored.

Miro came out from under canvas to take his phone call in the sun where he'd not be heard. He pressed the mobile to his ear to cut out the Tannoy commentary, and muttered, "I told Middleton to deal with it. What does he do all day?" He grimaced. "Don't tell me."

He stood feet astride on an unoccupied length of expensively rented river bank, his back to the marquee, his gaze across the shining river. "Fifty centimetres. Do what's necessary . . . I don't know. . . . I'm busy—what do I pay you people for? Use—your—initiative."

He clicked off the phone. He turned, startled, but it was only Joanna at his shoulder. She looked stunning in a formal but lightweight summer dress. She said, "Is it still too low?"

"Pathetic," he said. "I told them—if necessary, raise the RSJ."

"I meant the dress," she stammered. "You thought the front was too revealing."

He chuckled. "I can never see enough of you!"

"Oh. Well. Yes, that supermarket—the doorway's still not high enough?"

"Just because some stupid supplier has non-standard trucks."

"It shouldn't be difficult," she said.

Miro looked anxious. "I don't know. We may have to tell the client he can't accept their trucks. He'll go ballistic."

He had one eye on the marquee and he suddenly waved and smiled to someone inside. Jo was carrying an unnecessary pair of sheer summer gloves which she tapped impatiently on one hand. She wanted to be helpful. "Is there really no way you can raise the height of the entrance?"

"Apparently not. Ridiculous."

"And they can't lower the delivery trucks by deflating the tyres?"

He shrugged impatiently. "Four or five centimetres. That's no use."

"Can't you lower the floor?"

"What?" He laughed shortly.

She screwed up her gloves. "Leave the wall as it is and dig out the tarmac to make a dip. Is that possible?"

Miro stared at her. "It wouldn't be elegant," he said.

"It's the back of the building," she said. "Who'd see—except the lorry drivers?"

"It needn't be a sharp dip," he muttered, lifting his phone again. "One more favour, darling. Pop back to the marquee and make sure no one comes over for the next minute or so. Get Florian to help you."

"I can manage," she said, moving away, blushing with pleasure because she knew she had suggested something useful.

Miro gazed at his fiancée's back as she slipped to the marquee, then he pressed Redial on the phone. "Me again," he said gruffly. "That Goods Inwards door. Got a solution yet? Well, I've had an idea."

She had become bored in the tent. There was only one other woman—and she was dressed like a man and talking business. Miro was pouring champagne. What was the point of coming to this beautiful spot, paying a fortune for the marquee, and then just talking shop? Joanna went out and sat on the grass beside the river. On either side she could see into other corporate enclosures along the bank. Some of the lawns were empty, while in others small groups of men stood with glasses in their hands, casually watching the boat races. Two sculls shot past, each driven by a single oarsman drenched in water. She had no idea what the race was or who to support, but watching the boats was more interesting than standing dutifully in the marquee. The sunshine, the blue river, the occasional flash of men in white. Lovely to look at but too soon gone. She grinned. She was at peace here by herself.

"I don't know why half these people come," a voice said.

She spun round. It was Florian. He shouldn't be here in the corporate enclosure. He was a driver—even if he was wearing one of those ridiculous striped Henley blazers. Where on earth had he got that?

"You and I," he said. "The only ones to see it."

"See what?" she asked stupidly. She couldn't deal with him.

"Those men on the river," he continued. "Sweating their guts out. All year they've trained for this, then the spectators turn their backs."

"Shouldn't you be with the car?"

He kept the good side of his face towards her. "They eat, they chatter, they drink free champagne—and they think they've been to Henley. But they haven't been here at all."

Seen from this side he looked quite normal. But she knew better. "You're not allowed to drink, are you? You're the driver."

"It's too hot to drink. A day like this, one should sit on the river bank and watch young men stripped to their T-shirts. Yes?"

He had the nerve to lean down to her, and she snapped, "I'm not in the mood for talking, thank you."

But he sat beside her on the dry grass, still showing his unblemished side. "Let's sit here, you and I, the only ones to enjoy what the world can offer."

She stiffened. "You should be guarding the car."

He ignored that. "You and I don't fit here."

She stood up. "I don't know where you fit."

Everything about the man irritated her. Not just his face—he couldn't help that—but his insinuating manner, his assumed friendliness, even his well-modulated voice. Where had he learned to speak like that? He spoke as if he'd been educated in a private school—yet he was nothing more than a chauffeur. He was affected, that was all—putting on airs.

Perhaps he was well educated. Perhaps his ruined face prevented him from getting on in life—so that all he could get was a menial job like this. At least it put him back in touch with money, and allowed him to drive a fancy car. But she didn't care. She wasn't interested in Florian. She walked to the marquee.

At the river bank, Florian glanced briefly across his shoulder, and because she didn't look back he continued watching. He wanted her. He couldn't help wanting her. From the corner of his eye he noticed her white sheer gloves left behind on the green grass. Gloves, when the temperature was eighty. A tailor-made frock, the gloves, impractical shoes—she tried so hard. But why did she dress as if she were in her mid-thirties? She tried to dress upper class—tried to be upper class. But Miro wasn't upper, he just had money. People with money didn't have to act any way at all. Didn't she realise that she only had to stand around looking beautiful?

He glanced again at her gloves. If he took them across to her she'd only snap at him: "Who asked you to pick them up?" He looked at the marquee. In the gloom beneath the canvas she had found old Miro, and was smiling up at him as he held forth to one of his boring fat rich clients. She's like his daughter, thought Florian, his favoured child.

Florian picked up her gloves. She wasn't watching him. And what if she was? Let her see him. He raised the gloves to his face and inhaled their smell. She may not have worn them—except, yes, she'd worn them earlier, in the car. Dressed up for her outing. When he breathed in deeply he could smell her perfume. Perhaps she'd sprayed the gloves— the perfume may not have come directly from her skin. But it was her fragrance. She had worn them.

Florian slipped his hand into one glove. He mustn't push too far because his hand was too large. It would stretch them. But if he was careful he could slip his fingers into something personal of hers, something warm—though it was just the warmth of a hot summer's day he felt, not her warmth. But the gloves, yes, she had worn them. They were her. Slowly, he introduced his fingers into Joanna's finger sockets. His big masculine fingers in her tight feminine sockets. He mustn't push too hard. This soft silky material would stretch to admit him, embrace him, but it might not snap back. He might push the sockets out of shape. Then they'd never go back as they had been before. They'd be spoiled. And what would she say? If he thrust his fingers into her delicate fleshy nooks, she was cruel enough to want his skin flayed and made into a pair of winter gloves.

Chapter 3

Florian drove the Lexus with one finger. He slumped in the buff leather driving seat, window open, arm outside, his hand barely resting on the wheel. Joanna sat in the back and, for the first time, the streets out there looked different. They looked dusty. People seemed cheaply dressed and careworn. Yet it was such a lovely day. The sun had shone ten days without a break but, perhaps because it was the end of their working day, the people did not look grateful.

She had liked this street once. When she first moved here, her own flat, she had shivered with joy at being able to have her own place in a tree-lined street among real families. Now it looked dull.

Florian asked, "Are you going to keep the flat? I haven't seen a For Sale sign."

"I rent it."

She didn't think she'd miss the flat—but it was her place, somewhere she could be alone. It had been important to her once, when she first left home. She had needed somewhere private. The biggest change in marrying Miro might be the loss of this bolt-hole. Most couples when they married moved into somewhere new to both of them. But she would be joining Miro in his existing place. Compared to her little flat, Miro's fine country house was a palace. She had stayed there often—in these recent weeks stayed very often—but she had kept her little hideaway. Soon her life would be like spending every day in a grand hotel.

Florian said, "Just over a week to the wedding. I suppose you'll spend the next few nights here on your own?"

"Probably."

"You should. These last few days it isn't right for you to *live* with Miro. Your wedding day should mark a change in your life."

"I didn't know you were so sentimental."

They were driving into Pinehurst, one of Swindon's large housing estates.

"You don't want every day to be the same as the one before."

Jo's flat was upstairs in a little two-storey house: brick downstairs, concrete above. Most houses had small, neglected gardens. One or two hedges had been rooted up to create hard standing for the car, but most cars still parked on the road.

While Florian looked for a parking space he noticed a man lounging against the brick pillar to Jo's gate. He glanced in his mirror and saw that she had seen him too. She said hurriedly, "Anywhere will do. Somewhere up there."

She indicated a space thirty yards on. When she got out, clutching her small overnight bag, she said, "That'll do. You needn't wait."

Florian checked his mirror again. The young man was watching them. Jo said, "Thank you. Goodbye."

She wanted to see him go.

Florian nodded. "You'll be all right?"

"Of course. Don't be late for Miro."

Florian pulled away. He didn't need to fetch Miro till six o'clock. He drove slowly up the street, one eye ahead and one on the mirror. Joanna was walking slowly. The young man was still beside her gate.

The street continued past a triangular playing area the length of a football pitch. Florian turned left beside it, drove fifty yards, and paused. She didn't want me to see him, he thought. A week before her wedding that's not surprising, because he isn't here to discuss church flowers. He is not a preacher. So who is he—her best man?

Florian decided not to burst in on the happy couple. He'd give them time to say hello.

He looked at his watch. Plenty of time.

When she opened the door Florian said, "Me again," and barged straight in. Ignoring her protests he chose the first open door—the sitting room, lounge, call it what she will: the room with her manky furniture, cheap stuff she'd leave behind when she married Miro. The room with the young man standing by the television, the young man who hadn't reached the bedroom. Yet.

The man snarled, "The hell are you?"

Florian stared at him. The man stared back. Jo came into the room and snapped, "What on earth d'you think you're doing?"

"Looking for explanations."

The young guy had short sandy hair. He took a step forward. He looked usefully built but so was Florian.

Jo stamped her foot, "How dare you?"

"Who is this man?"

"The fuck is this?" the man asked.

"Your name?"

Jo said, "Get out," which had as much effect as shouting at the wall.

"I want to know who this man is."

"She told you to get out. You hear that?"

27

"This could take a long time," said Florian. "But if you like, I'll speed things up."

Jo said, "This is an old friend of mine from school." She stammered slightly. "His name is Alan Pirie. I'm allowed to see my friends."

Alan said, "Who the fuck are you?"

"You're her boyfriend?"

"I said who the fuck are you?"

"You know she's getting married?"

"Is she?" Alan glanced at Jo. "Well, that's no surprise. You the lucky feller?"

"I am her fiancée's chauffeur."

Alan shook his head. "What is this crap?"

Jo said, "Please go now. You've done enough."

"Chauffeur!" Alan laughed. "That's rich."

Florian stared at him. "You're not rich, are you?"

Alan stared back. Florian said, "Miss Beattie is marrying my boss. But I find you here in her flat. That doesn't look good."

"I don't give a stuff how it looks."

"Say what you have to, then we can go."

"Sod off and mind the car."

Florian stepped forward. Jo cried, "Florian! Stop it. You must go—now."

He turned to her slowly. "You want him to stay?"

"It's nothing. He's just a friend."

"Is that what I am to tell Miro?"

She didn't know what to say. But Florian knew that from here on, the more he tried to stay the more *he* would be in the wrong. He would have to leave.

He said, "We'll talk later," and left the room.

Chapter 4

Morning. Nine o'clock. Florian stands outside the door to Joanna's flat, bright and shining as if he has shaved, and he peers over her shoulder to see inside.

"I'll get my bag," she says.

"No hurry."

When she turns away, Florian steps inside the little hall. She says, "Wait. I'm coming."

"Can I use your loo?"

She stares at him. "You don't want that. You just want to pry."

He is in now. Throwing his hands wide. "Pry?"

She hates his put-on accent. "I'm not stupid. Wait outside."

"Something to hide?"

She picks up her bag. "Let's go."

He doesn't move. "This is very foolish."

"Don't push it."

"He's in your bedroom?"

"Who? No one is."

"Joanna."

Her eyes blaze. "Who gave you the right to—to use my first name?"

Those eyes. She looks beautiful. He says, "Even Miro lets me call him Miro."

"He's your boss."

"Anything special he wants done—"

"I'm your boss too."

"Can a servant serve two masters? What would you like me to tell Miro?"

"Nothing. We'll be late."

"I came early. The man's still here, then?"

"No one is."

"I'd better look."

It was a victory for both of them. But whenever both win, neither can be satisfied. She showed him around the flat defiantly, glaring into each little room. First she showed the sitting room, but that wasn't where he'd be. Then the bathroom, in case she had hidden him in there. When she opened the door to the bedroom she said "See?" and stamped to the hall. But Florian went to the bed.

"Do look underneath," she called sarcastically.

The bed was made, its duvet pulled up roughly to meet a heap of crumpled pillows. Florian fingered the material to her coverlet. "What time did he go?"

"He only stayed about half an hour."

"You're sure?" Florian still had hold of the duvet. His fingers moved and squeezed the material as if it had been her dress. "Half an hour?"

He had a gleam in his eye, as if he knew better. For all she knew he might have waited in the street last night. "Maybe a bit longer. An hour, I'm not sure."

"What did you talk about?"

"For God's sake! Look, I proved you wrong. He isn't here."

"Did you go to bed with him?"

Her eyes blazed again. He loved the life in those eyes. She wouldn't answer. Before she could turn to leave, Florian threw back the duvet to expose the sheet. He examined it. No stains.

"What the hell d'you think you're doing?"

He didn't reply. She watched him run his hand across her sheet. Then he stooped, placed his nose against it and breathed in deeply. He raised his head and held the smell to analyse it like a connoisseur. He lowered his head again and rubbed his face against other parts of her sheet, breathing in each time.

"How dare you?" she gasped. He smiled at her. She almost spat. "Smell anything you shouldn't smell?"

"Only you, Joanna. You're not in trouble, are you—loose ends from the past?"

"No."

"Loose ends can be aggravating. But if you need a hand, I'm always here."

She snorted. Florian was the last person she would turn to.

Joanna and Dee were waiting outside Miro's office. Jo muttered, "Look at him strutting."

"Who?"

"That . . . chauffeur. He's an animal."

Dee laughed. "He's built like an animal."

Joanna said nothing. She left Dee at the office entrance, stomped to the Lexus and climbed inside. It was hot in the back. Florian leant in and said, "I'll switch on the air con."

She ignored him. Miro arrived with Dee, who was now clutching at the sleeve of a tall man from Miro's office. He joshed with Miro: "I hear you have a prior claim on this gorgeous young lady."

Florian switched on the air conditioning. It wasn't loud but it made it harder for Jo to hear the others chattering out-

31

side. She heard the tall man: "You don't work for us, so what do you do?"

"I do very nicely!" said Dee with a laugh.

"I bet."

She laughed again. He said, "Whereabouts do you live?"

"Old Town."

"That's right on my way."

Miro hooted. The man said, "I'll give you a lift, Dee. No point bothering Miro."

"Not today, thank you, sir," laughed Dee in her best telephone manner, and she scrambled into the Lexus to join Joanna in the rear.

Miro said, "That's put you in your place, Jasper!"

He walked round to get in the front.

Jo whispered, "Jasper! You're kidding."

"I know. Isn't it a wonderful name?"

"Why didn't you go with him?"

Dee tossed her head. "Too public." The car started forward. "But I gave him my phone number!"

They drove Dee to her flat. Florian wondered about Dee: blonde hair was exciting, and she was a pert little number—brassy, upfront. Working in telephone sales left her always on the go, a bright reflex smile, fast with her words, but a bit mechanical, he thought. Always helpful, always positive, as if she had her script off by heart. She'd look the same on the telephone, he thought: her plastic headset would disappear into that mop of blonde hair and she'd chatter gaily, hard eyed, just as she did now in real life. What did she see in Jasper? She was a party animal, clubbing and disco, while Jasper was at least ten years older, would hate disco and the only clubs he'd know would be used for golf. Ten years older: maybe she was aping her friend, having seen what a good catch her school friend had made. Jo had been an office girl, a clerk in Vermont Era, but her superb looks had made her stand out. It was a small office and Miro had never really got over the death of his first wife, and he'd whisked Joanna Beattie from her humdrum existence into his. She must have thought she'd won the lottery. Instead of a two-room flat in Pinehurst she would have a palace. It must seem that way to her.

And to Dee. When they dropped her she put her head back inside the window and wished them all a bright goodbye— and thank you, Miro, for such a really lovely day. Then she spun away sharply as if cutting them off for her next phone call. Florian glanced at her once before easing the car forward: scheming little bitch. Wondering how she could join the rich set. Wondering how much money Jasper earned.

Jo was speaking, so he tuned in.

"Too much sun."

Miro asked, "You've had an aspirin?"

"Paracetamol. I'll be happier in my own bed."

Miro chuckled. "You have your own bed at the house."

"I have my own *half*."

"You'll be miserable in that little flat, darling."

"I'll be better there. Honestly."

Honesty, thought Florian, is in short supply. She may have a headache or she may not, but if she's in her own flat she is out of sight. If she's in her own flat she can do what she likes—see who she likes. And last night she saw a young man—a school friend, who happened to drop by, who she hadn't seen for a couple of years, who didn't mean anything. A young man it wasn't worth mentioning to Miro.

Honesty, he thought. Is Joanna honest? He wished that he knew what had happened in her flat last night. They had not been old school friends swapping memories. Jo might have insisted it was innocent, but both men seemed to have a hold on her. Miro certainly had, and this other man? She couldn't be innocent and please both of them. If she betrayed her husband now, before she had even wedded him, she'd do it again. And once they start . . .

Joanna let herself in to her Pinehurst flat. She dropped her bag against the wall, slipped out of her lightweight jacket and hung it up. She let out her breath. Small as the flat was, it was her own. Rented maybe, but her own. She could do as she wanted here, no one watching her, no one telling her what to do. This was *her* place—it might not be much but it was home. It would be a shame to lose it. Maybe Miro would let her keep it—the place didn't cost much, not by his standards. It could be her bolt-hole. Somewhere to get away.

She looked in the mirror in the hall. She had aged ten years. Anyone watching might have soothed her, said no, you're twenty, you've no bags or lines. But Jo could see the dryness, the faint bruising beneath the eyes. She looked as if she were at the height—or depth—of her period, but that had been last week. She had timed the wedding so that even if the monthly cycle slipped a little she would be clear for that big day. Twenty years old? She looked twenty-six. Ancient. Really old.

But staring at herself in the mirror would not cheer her up. She would make a coffee, flop in front of the telly and zombie out.

When she pushed the door to her living room Alan said, "Hello."

She gaped at him. He was the one who sat zombied out. He was stretched full length in her armchair, shoes off, bottle open, girlie magazine on the floor.

34

He said, "Thought you was never coming in. Fixing your make-up, was you?"

"What are you doing here?"

"Welcome home yourself."

He stared up at her from the chair.

"You can't do this, Alan."

"That's a nice posh frock you're wearing. He buy it for you?"

"Did you break in?"

She marched to the hall, but he called after her, "Nothing's broken. You just came through there yourself."

She stopped at the door and turned on him. "Look, I told you once. I'm not going through this again."

"That's it, is it—I don't have a say?"

"Don't pretend you're bothered."

"Bothered?" he roared, rising from the chair. "I came here special, didn't I?"

She shouted from the door. "That's right. Hoping to get your end away!"

"And did I? No. Did I force you or anything? No. Two years it's been."

"Exactly. Anything we had finished two years ago."

He stepped towards her. "You've had a life these last two years. I haven't."

"Whose fault was that?"

He exhaled loudly, then reached down for his beer. "I don't believe this," he muttered. "I thought you was waiting till I got out."

"Ha!" she shouted. "I'd want a jailbird! It's been two years, Alan."

He drank some beer. "You never liked sex anyway."

"Whose fault was that?"

He started for her, the bottle raised.

She yelled, "Go on, hit me! You've done that before."

"I never hit you."

"Oh, Christ."

She marched across the room and stared out the front window. An empty street. She had loved him once—the centre of her life.

He sniggered. "So this old guy—d'you have sex with him?"

She faced him. "Yes," she said.

He stared at her. "What's it like?"

She paused, knowing she could hurt him now. But she said, "Sex is sex, you know?"

He sniffed. "I just about remember."

"Oh, you'll find someone."

"Like I found you." He sounded plaintive. "You never came to see me, did you?"

Her voice rose. "Why should I? What had you ever done for me—except foul up my life?"

"Oh, that's nice, that's really nice." He stomped towards her. "I wrote to you."

"Yeah? I never got it."

"I wrote to your mum's place."

She snorted. "What d'you think she did with it? Chucked it in the bin."

"No, she likes me, your old mum."

"If she could've got a knife to you she'd have carved off your cock."

He was standing by her, less threatening now. "No, she likes me."

"Yeah? Go and see her, did you?"

"No," he mumbled.

"Just as well. Who gave you this address?"

He looked up. "Why? You in hiding or something?"

She frowned. "Who told you?"

"Dee did. Why?"

"Dee?"

"Ain't she supposed to? Christ, she's known me half my life. She knows I'm your boyfriend."

"That's rubbish."

He paused. "I said I was looking up old friends."

"Friends! We're not friends."

He took her elbow. "Listen. We had our problems, I know that."

"Problems!"

"We're still engaged, you know?"

"We are not!"

She broke away.

He raised his left hand. "I'm still wearing the ring."

She could smell the beer on him. "That's nothing."

"It's not nothing. I wore this ring all the time I was inside. I stayed true to you, Jo."

"Oh, in prison you had a choice?"

He grabbed her hand. "Where's your ring? This thing you're wearing ain't the one I bought you."

"This is a proper ring!" She ignored his reaction and continued hurriedly: "Don't give me that guff about being true to me. You were never true. We were finished before you ever went inside. You know that."

He mumbled, "Yeah? Then why did I wear your ring in jail?"

"To keep the queers away?"

"You're sick, you know that? We were special once."

"Oh, we were certainly special." She stared straight in his face. "You were the worst thing that ever happened to me."

"Well, thanks," he mumbled, dropping her hand and wandering away. "That was really worth waiting for. Makes the

37

last two years worth while."

"Don't act as if you went inside for me," she scoffed. "You were caught for stealing. You'd dumped me weeks before."

"Where's my ring, then—you chucked it away?"

He was backpedalling. She could see it, and she wouldn't flinch. "Yes, you dumped me, so I dumped your ring."

"But it's got our names on it. I'm still wearing yours."

"Throw it away, Alan. Start again."

He rubbed his ring, as if it had magic properties. "You can't marry that doddery old man."

"He's not old," she snapped. "Forget him. Forget me. Get a life."

"You can't marry him."

"Time to go, Alan."

"How rich is he?"

"Rich enough."

"He's got a chauffeur. I suppose he's got a big house?"

"Big enough."

"Yeah, well, I reckon perhaps you should marry him—then you can cut me in."

"Get real."

"I'm serious."

She strode past him into the little hall. "Here's the front door, Alan."

He wandered after her. "This ain't goodbye, you know," he said. "If you know what's good for you, you'll cut me a slice."

Chapter 5

When Florian collected Jo for lunch next morning he made no attempt to come inside the flat. He offered to carry her little overnight bag, but she ignored him and carried it herself—though when they reached the car she grudgingly allowed him to stow it away. While he did so she sat in the back as she always did, treating the Lexus as a taxi. Florian got in and started up.

"Feeling better today?"

"I feel fine."

"How are the neighbours?"

She rolled her eyes.

"Two or three times a week they see this big car pick you up. People must think you're a film star."

"Hardly."

"You do *talk* to the neighbours?"

She grunted, watching the houses go by. He'd get to the point soon.

"I wonder what they make of you."

She stared at the back of his head. He was an ominous, ugly man.

"From time to time an expensive car comes, and you get inside and disappear. No one else here drives a Lexus."

She didn't answer. He was the one who wanted dialogue.

He said, "But sometimes when you *are* here your boyfriend turns up."

"Are you staying with this?"

"I'm concerned for you."

"Making trouble, more like."

"You'll make trouble for yourself."

She snorted. "Keep on with this and I'll make trouble for *you*. Look Florian, every time you get me alone you start nagging at me. You sneer. You dig. Do you think I'll put up with that?"

"I only—"

"You think I'm frightened of my *chauffeur?*"

"Look—"

"You're threatening me, aren't you? You think I'm a kid. You think you can push me around."

He chuckled. "I don't think anyone—"

"Well, if I hear another word of this, if you try a single threat, I'm going straight to Miro and I'm going to—"

"I wouldn't do that."

"Oh, you wouldn't—d'you think I'm scared?"

"Nothing scares you."

"Don't get clever with me! You have a dirty, evil mind and I don't know why Miro puts up with you. Except you don't talk like this to him, do you? You wouldn't dare. But you think because I'm a girl you can say what you want. Well, I won't take it. If you want a fight I'll give you one—another word, one single word, I'll go straight to Miro. I'll have you sacked. Why should I care? I hate you. I won't let you ruin my life."

"Ruin you? I only want to help—"

"Shut up! From now on you do what I say. Right?"

"My goodness. Listening to you is like standing in a hail storm."

40

"I'm in charge here, right?"

"Pelt me with your stones!"

"You think it's funny?"

He chuckled again. "I'll tell you what is funny, Joanna: this is the first time you and I have really made contact."

"Contact?"

"It's the first time you've opened up to me."

After the business lunch it was blissfully silent in the car. Miro sat with his eyes closed, Florian watched the road and Jo wondered whether she should say something. She could wait till evening when she and Miro were alone or she could ignore Florian and speak now. In the world of Country Life, she thought, people of quality spoke unreservedly in front of servants. People waited on hand and foot had no alternative—servants were always there. And she did need to speak to Miro—preferably before they dropped him at his office. It shouldn't wait until evening.

She said, "Are you awake?"

"Always."

"I'm sorry I was beastly over lunch."

He opened his eyes. "In what way?"

"I was rude to your colleagues—"

"They're not colleagues, darling, they're clients. Sources of income."

She smiled back. "I felt . . . unnecessary."

"Patronised, I expect. Don't worry—they were both furious with jealousy." He smiled again and touched her hand. "Did me the world of good."

"I thought I'd let you down."

"No, you were haughty. You were magnificently icy with them."

"I'm sorry."

"I loved it. They had no more chance of patronising you than of sleeping with you."

"No chance!"

"See? You're gorgeous when you're angry. I bet they're talking about you now."

"I hope not."

"Saying how sensational you are."

She chuckled shyly. "I'm not."

"You've no idea. When you get on that high horse we men just fall aside. All the blood drains from your face. Two little spots of red appear high in your cheek and your eyes shine like a vengeful Madonna. Yes, you showed such disdain I could have eaten you."

She snuggled in to him. He made her feel safe.

She whispered, "I'm glad we're getting married."

After they had dropped Miro at the office she knew Florian would start.

"Difficult lunch, eh?"

She grunted. She sat right in the corner to stop him catching her eye in the rear view mirror.

He said, "Makes you wonder how some people can be so lucky. It can't just be age."

She nodded slightly but said nothing.

"Funny, isn't it? People our age are much the same. We've hardly any money yet, no power, but over the next ten years we'll fly apart like shrapnel. Some of us will never have money, others will shoot to the top, and all the rest will end up somewhere in between. If you look at us now, though, our generation, our lives ahead of us, you can't tell who'll end up where. D'you ever think about that?"

"No."

"Don't you ever wonder what will happen?"

Jo shrugged. She couldn't look at him: his fearful scar was facing her. He said, "Well, as I've told you before, Joanna, you have plenty of business lunches to look forward to."

She glanced out the window. They had driven out of town.

He said, "All those tedious businessmen. I wonder how long Miro will let you be so icy with them. He could get tired of it. It might not always seem magnificent."

"Just stick to the driving."

"I wish I'd been there, though—to see you on your high horse. Yes, you're gorgeous when you're angry." He drawled the words, then laughed.

She snapped, "I've had enough of this."

"I'm joking with you."

"I don't want it. I don't want you nagging at me. If you keep this up you'll be out of a job."

"I nag because I care for you."

"That's enough!"

"Care about you, I should say."

"Stop the car."

"I'm always at your service—"

"Stop the car!"

"I will not."

"What?"

"I won't stop the car in the middle of nowhere. What for?"

"I'm getting out."

"Here? You're joking!"

He didn't even alter speed. She grabbed the door handle.

He said, "Don't be foolish, Jo. You'll get hurt."

She opened the door. He slammed the brakes. As the car slowed she pushed it wider. The car stopped.

Jo jumped out and stood beside the car. They were in a quiet unbending lane in which the only sound was the car engine. Beside her, the grass looked overlong and limp with heat. Cow parsley swayed above the verges, and creamy blobs of elderflower drooped from the trees. Florian had his window down, and he looked at her with faint amusement.

She said, "You can go now."

He chuckled. "And leave you here?"

"I'll walk home. I've had enough."

"In this heat—and those shoes? It'll take an hour."

"I'm walking."

To prove it she walked on beyond the car. Florian eased forward and cruised at walking speed beside her. She could see the good side of his face now—he looked perfectly acceptable as he leant from the window. "We could go on for ages like this."

"Sod off."

"That's my Joanna."

She stopped and turned on him. "You've lost your job, mister."

"You're not my boss."

"Oh yes, I am."

"Jo, it's far too hot for this today. Come back inside the car."

"No way."

"You can't walk all the way to the house."

"It'll only take an hour."

"Look, I'm sorry. I apologise. I was only trying to help, but if you don't want my help, I won't offer it again."

"That's it? No more nagging, no more cheek?"

"You're the boss. In the future I shall behave as if you really were my mistress!"

She flared up. "That's exactly what I mean! You twist everything. This is never going to work."

"Joanna." Florian stepped lightly from the car and stood

in the lane beside her. "We must come to an understanding, you and I."

Beneath the trees the air was hot and unmoving. He stood so she couldn't see his bad side. She said, "There's nothing to understand. This isn't going to work."

"What isn't?"

"I don't trust you."

He reached out a hand but checked himself and leant instead against the car. "I think we can make it work," he said.

"No."

"Don't turn me away."

She stared at him. In the balmy air she could smell the sweet heavy scent of elderflower. "It's too late," she said.

"It's too hot. I can't let you walk."

"No? Well, I'm not getting back in that car with you. I'll walk—it isn't far."

He breathed out. "D'you feel how hot it is? There's no breeze today. The air is absolutely still. Everything's played out, like you and I."

He reached out but she stepped back.

He said, "Please. Get in the car. Things will be different now."

"I don't believe you. No."

"Can't you trust me?"

She shook her head.

Florian said, "I can't touch you in the car. But you know, out here in this lonely lane, these empty fields, you would not be safe at all. If I were to take hold of you here, what could you do?"

"Take hold . . . What d'you mean?"

"You're not an innocent, Jo. You know exactly what I mean."

45

She stared at him. He said, "Shall I walk beside you, side by side?"

"No!"

"In that field, on the other side of the hedge, no one could see us."

"They'd see the car."

The smile looked weird on his crippled face. "You're afraid someone might see us?"

"I don't know what you're talking about. I'm going home."

"I'll walk with you. Across the fields or along the lane?"

"You can't—"

Jo stopped, unsure what she wanted to say. She said, "You can't leave the Lexus."

He nodded. "Then you'd better get inside."

Jo shook her head.

"No what?" he whispered.

"I don't trust you."

"I see that."

"Give me the key."

He frowned at her.

She said, "You don't want me to walk, so you walk. I'll drive the car."

When she looked inside she could see the key in the ignition. She said, "You're in my way."

"Want me to move?"

"Yes." She and Florian stood a yard apart. "Please."

He inclined his head and stepped aside.

In the narrow space between the Lexus and the hedgerow she had to brush against him to get inside. She slipped into his seat and held her breath. He didn't move. Jo started the car. As the Lexus pulled away she could see Florian in the rearview mirror, standing motionless in the middle of the green and empty lane. He was staring after her.

Chapter 6

As the gates of Electra Court swung closed behind the Lexus, Jo realised that this was the first time she had arrived to an empty house. She had occasionally been left by herself when Florian had taken Miro to work but she had never arrived unaccompanied. She had always been brought by Florian or Miro. She had never experienced silent arrival—had never been able to drift into the house alone and unwind. She stopped the car on the cobbles at the foot of the wide front steps and sat for a moment looking out across the sun-baked grounds. This would become another part of her life—arriving back at her own home. Driving in without a thought because she lived here. Letting herself in at her own front door. Treating the place as her own.

No one else to deal with.

She leant across the steering wheel to peer up at the house. In the bright sunlight the old grey Cotswold stone had turned dusty apricot and the mullioned windows sparkled darkly like antique mirrors. Once there would have been servants awaiting her arrival. No sooner would she have pulled up outside the house than the door would have opened and at least one servant would have run down the steps to welcome her home. "Bring my bag," she'd say—no, she wouldn't have had to say a thing; they would have done it naturally. It wouldn't have occurred to anyone that the lady of the house should carry her own bag. Someone would have parked the car. Someone else would have brought her tea.

It was odd to think of waiting in a drawing room for tea to arrive—rather like being in an upmarket hotel where you had to rely on Room Service. But Electra Court wasn't a hotel, it would be her home. Large as it was, she would learn to treat it as she treated her flat—to wander into her own kitchen, open her cupboards, take out her own favourite brand of tea, put on the kettle, fetch milk from the fridge. Just like home. She smiled at the thought of such domestic pleasures.

First, of course, she must park the car.

She drove around the side of the house to where the cars were garaged in the converted stable block. There was room for four cars, though Miro owned only two. The stables ran in a line to one side of and behind the main house, and at the end of the block was where Miro had placed the annex. He was proud of his innovative annex design, though Jo thought it too bold and out of keeping. Miro had forsworn any attempt to meld with the other eighteenth century buildings. He hadn't even constructed it with Cotswold stone.

She barely glanced at it as she manoeuvred the Lexus into an open garage, its sudden shade a surprise after the unremitting glare outside. When she got out she was aware of the car's heat in the cool garage, like a radiator left on by mistake. She left the deep shade of the converted stable and waited while the garage door closed automatically. Sunlight glinted from the glass frontage of the annex. It was shaped rather like a glass marquee, glass and white UPVC, designed by Miro to recall a huge Georgian orangery. Immediately inside the glass was a real conservatory but behind that frontage ran a line of rooms. The main glass door from outside opened onto a short, tiled path straight through the conservatory into the private suite behind. The rooms were multi-functional—one as a bedroom but the other three for use either as meeting rooms or small chambers. In two of those rooms a dividing wall could fold away to make a single conference hall, in which Miro had installed expensive audio-visual equipment for client presentations. Since Jo had known him he had used it only once.

She walked back round the side of the house, carrying her overnight case in her hand and her handbag over one shoulder. The sun beat down on her head and she thought how ridiculous it would have been to attempt that hour-long walk home. Just climbing the steps brought her out in sweat. At the top of the steps she rested the case and reached in her handbag for the key.

He said, "I've been dying for a cup of tea."

She spun round. He was in a recess at the foot of the steps. Disentangling himself, as if he had been cramped in there so long that his body had grown stiff, Alan emerged into full sunlight. Though the brightness made him blink he tried a nonchalant grin. He had surprised her, as he'd intended.

"On your own, I'm glad to see."

She stared at him, not wanting to ask the obvious question—how had he found Miro's house? He was standing at the foot of the steps. If she was smart with her key she could push the door open and be inside before he got to her. Then what? Have him hammering at the door and pretend she couldn't hear?

"Have you been waiting long?" she asked, her voice cold and under control.

He climbed the steps to join her. "Long enough to get a look round."

He was wearing an ordinary shirt—too heavy, with the sleeves rolled to his elbows. His trousers were heavy. Perhaps he had no summer clothes.

49

She let her bag hang loose, the key still safe inside. "You were lucky," she said.

"Mm?"

"You picked a time no one's in." She met him on the steps and continued down them.

"Where're you going?"

Get him on the back foot, she thought, as she reached the cobbles. She raised a hand lazily and gestured at the grounds. "You know these country properties. No, I suppose you don't."

"Don't get posh with me, girl." He glared after her but had to follow her down.

She said, "Out here they shoot intruders."

He was beside her as she wandered to the rose border. "Don't give me that," he said.

"It's a different world, you know? Hunting, culling, shooting grouse. You saw the gamekeeper?"

"Don't give me that. There's no one—just you and me."

She gazed at him blankly. In this remote house perhaps Miro's shotguns were not such a silly idea. Alan looked uncomfortable in his cheap town clothes. His lanky blond hair clung to his head. She said, "You don't carry a gun, do you?"

"Do me a—"

"After your time in prison I though you might."

He shook his head and tried to smile. "I'm not going for this."

"Good," she said, tapping him on the arm. "I'm glad you don't have a gun."

She had unsettled him enough that she could begin to wander along the drive beside the rose bed. He called, "Ain't you gonna invite me in the house?"

"Oh look, my goodness—black spot."

"What?"

50

She smiled at him in the sun. "On this bush."

This was going too far. "Don't act Lady Muck with me!"

"Black spot is more of a problem here than in town. Traffic pollution kills it there."

He grabbed her arm. "Any more and I'll knock your block off."

"You were always good at it." She smiled at him. "I suppose you're on parole?"

He stared at her. She said, "You shouldn't have come, should you?"

"You've grown up, Jo."

"Did you drive here?"

He was floundering as she continued switching subjects. He muttered, "Yeah, it's round the side—"

"I suppose you stole it?"

"Well, borrowed it. So what?"

She shook her head reprovingly. "The police are going to love you."

He actually stamped his foot. "Christ! Are you fucking serious?"

"What d'you expect?"

"You're supposed to be my friend."

"Friend?" She made herself keep her voice calm. "This is not a friendly visit, Alan."

"Why not?"

"You'd better leave before the others arrive."

"Oh no. This is your house, right?"

"No."

"All right, clever, not yet it's not. But you live here."

"I live in Pinehurst."

"Don't give me that! You fucking live here, so you're allowed to invite a friend in."

She tried to throw him again. "Where did you put your car?"

He was getting wise to her now. "I'm coming in."

"Not possible."

"Everything's fucking possible." He nodded at the house. "You better get this in your head, girl—I know where you live. I can come here anytime."

"Not sensible."

"And don't give me that guff about a gamekeeper and his gun. I been round this house and there ain't no gamekeeper. But it's a nice big house, Jo. I can see why you're marrying him."

Both of them were sweating in the sun. "Christ, it's hot," he said. "Let's go inside and have a cup of tea."

She glanced down the drive toward the gate, but it was too soon for Florian to arrive. An hour's walk, he'd said. Unless he had run.

She pointed across the lawn. "See the fountain? That's fresh water."

"What you think I am?" he roared. "A fucking animal? I get the horse trough?"

She headed for the fountain. "I drink it," she said. "It's nice."

She walked across the baking lawn towards the sparkling fountain. Made of reconstituted Cotswold stone and from the same mould as one Miro had installed outside a Wiltshire golf club, the Three Graces burbled prettily all summer. Miro admitted it was kitsch but said he liked the way the water trickled across the Graces' sinuous curves. It made their bodies seem quite lifelike. Stone became flesh.

Jo sat on the rim of the bowl around the statue and dipped her hands into the water. It felt wonderfully cool. Ignoring Alan, she splashed water across her face, then drank some greedily. She felt its coldness running through her veins. She shouldn't be out in this hot sun.

Alan said, "Come on, Jo, let's go in the house."

"Try some. It's only tap water."

She looked up at him and smiled pleasantly for the first time. She could see he was hot. Anyone would be. She left her hand trailing in the clear cool water. As close as this, she could smell it. The water made a gentle trickling sound. Alan started forward and scooped water in both hands. He drank noisily, then refilled his hands and drank again. He stared at her. She smiled. His shoulders dropped and suddenly he bent down and ducked his head in the bubbling water. He bent again and held his head beneath the surface for several seconds. When he came up he shook himself like a dog.

He grinned at her. "Well, at least you didn't hold me head under."

"Would I do that?"

He shook his head again. "I did wonder."

"You might as well sit down. It's nice here." Nice and near the gate, she thought, for when Florian finally gets back. "I suppose I have changed," she said. "Two years is a long time. At our age."

"Tell me about it," he said bitterly. "I really did think we'd get married, Jo."

"Don't start that again. I don't want to hurt you—but it's over, isn't it?"

He sat on the fountain and looked across the lawn toward the fine stone house. "Like, you mean, compared to this, I got nothing to offer you."

She nodded. He had nothing, he was nothing. He was a stranger now.

"Just comes down to money, don't it?"

"Don't build a fantasy, Alan. We were finished before you even went inside."

"I still want you, girl."

She glanced hopefully toward the gate. But it was too early yet. She stared at the water. "We can't go through this every time we meet, Alan. I hope you find someone. I wish you well. I'd like to think you could wish me well too."

He raised a wet hand from the fountain. "I'm still wearing your ring."

"I told you—"

"When are you marrying this guy?"

"Next week."

He flinched. "That's nice." He dropped his fingers back into the water. "No, you can't do this, Jo."

"You suggest I give this up—the house, money, all of that?"

"Does he know about our baby?"

There was silence. Not even a bird called. Then Jo sighed. Alan simply would not let go.

He said, "You're so young, he probably thinks you're a virgin."

"Of course he doesn't."

"Well, he knows you ain't virgin now."

"You can be so childish, you know that?"

"You want childish?" He splashed her with cold water from the fountain. She gasped. "That's childish. I bet you're childish with him. I bet he likes that."

She stood up. "That's enough. You'd better go now."

He reached out to grab her wrist. "You haven't told him about it, have you?"

"Let go of me," she said quietly.

His face looked pinched and ugly. "So if I tell him, that'll fuck your marriage?"

"He never thought that I was virgin."

"But he don't know about us—the three of us."

She shook her hand free. "There aren't three of us, only

54

one. Me. I'm the only one he cares about."

Alan stood up. "You're the only one he knows about."

Her face was angry now. "Listen. I wasn't virgin, right? He knows that. So he knows there must have been someone—but he doesn't waste his time trying to put a face to it. He's not a sad case like you."

"He won't mind if I tell him, then?"

"You would, wouldn't you? And then what? I fall into your arms saying, 'Oh Alan, I loved you all the time!' Live in the real world. Get a life."

She walked away across the lawn.

He followed. "It was my baby. We should be bringing it up together."

She spun on him. "Oh, puh-lease! Give me a break. You don't even know if it was a girl or a boy."

"I was in prison, I wasn't there!"

"You wouldn't have been there anyway—"

"I wanted it—"

"You only wanted sex." She glared up at the sun. "Leave it, Alan. Get in your stolen car and drive home."

He caught up with her. They stood incongruously beside the rose bed as he said, "We're bound together, you and me."

She looked away in irritation. "We were finished before you went to jail."

"No—"

"I was pregnant and you disappeared."

"I was busy. Anyway, after I was nicked I had time to think about it."

"Thanks."

"I wrote you, didn't I? Told you how I felt."

She caught his eye a moment, then turned to fiddle with a crumbly red rose. "I never got the letter."

"Letters. There was more than one. Christ, your mother—

didn't she pass them on?"

The roses were drooping in the heat. She said, "What's done is done."

Alan reached out beside her and snapped the head of a faded flower. "We can start again."

Like him, she began pulling the heads of dying roses. "You went into jail and left me pregnant. But even if you hadn't been caught you'd have left me anyway. You never wrote.— Whatever." She shrugged off his interruption, plucking at the roses. "Next thing I knew I was fifteen weeks gone. I still hadn't told my mother and I had to find some way to get an abortion. Fast."

She continued deadheading roses. "There was this doctor down in Bristol. I had to lie about the dates. I doubt if he believed me, though. Fifteen weeks gone, I reckoned. Nearly twenty by the time it was done. So the abortion was messy and painful. I do mean painful, Alan—the muck went on for weeks." She tugged at a rose. "It ruined sex with anyone."

"Even now?"

"Oh, not now," she said defensively.

He almost sneered. "I suppose the old guy's nice and gentle with you?"

"Thanks for the sympathy."

"Oh, yeah, it must have been tough."

She waited for more. He looked away, then said, "So you're OK now?"

"Hunky dory."

He fiddled with a dangling branch. "Good. What are we gonna do?"

"About what?"

"This . . . guy you're supposed to be marrying."

"The man I am marrying next week."

Alan shook his head. "You can't do that. Some old man."

56

"He's not an old man. I—I love him. I'm sorry."

"Love him? Come on, he's rich, ain't he?"

"That isn't it."

He laughed sharply. "What is he—good in bed?"

"Sex isn't everything."

"You mean he ain't no good in bed!"

"I mean sex isn't everything. It's overrated, if you want my opinion."

"Look, if he's not good enough—"

"Oh, do shut up. Listen, sex is all very well but it isn't earth shattering. It's not like the movies."

"No, not with some old guy—"

"He isn't old! Sex is the same with anyone. It was never earth-shattering with you."

Alan snatched at a rose and pricked his hand. "Ouch. No, come on. It was good, Jo, 'course it was. You and me could make it good again."

"No," she said slowly. "We can't make it good again. It's like your hand. Look, it's bleeding."

Alan glanced at his fingers. Blood ran freely from the scratch. "Don't marry him, Jo. You got to give me a chance."

She snorted in exasperation and walked away along the rose bed. Alan licked his blood. "I won't let you marry him."

She glanced across the lawns, on through the gate. Where was Florian? Why wasn't he back yet? "You sound pathetic," she muttered.

"Don't talk to me like that!"

She ignored him and continued to walk away. But he rushed up to her and grabbed feebly at her shoulder. When she pulled away he left a smear of blood across her dress.

Alan said, "I'm going to tell that bloke you had my baby."

"I didn't have it."

"No, you had it aborted. I'll tell him that."

She glanced at the shoulder of her dress. "That's your blood," she observed slowly.

Chapter 7

Cold water removes a bloodstain. Her mother had told her that. When Jo held the dress under a stream of cold water it darkened the colour of the material and she couldn't tell whether the stain had gone or not. The dress was supposed to be Dry Clean Only but didn't they all say that nowadays, to protect the manufacturer? She couldn't wait for her dress to be drycleaned. She rubbed some Shout into the shoulder where the stain had been, then threw the damp dress into the washing machine. It seemed wasteful to run the machine for one light summer dress. She wondered whether to make up the weight with bits and pieces of other washing. Oh, forget it, she thought. Just start the bloody machine. The bloodless machine, she hoped.

She pressed the Start button and waited in front of the machine as if standing guard beside it. She was shaking. The scene with Alan had unnerved her more than she had realised. He meant nothing to her and yet he had kept on about how they were meant for each other and how if they worked at it they could make everything all right. He really did think there was a chance she'd give Miro up for him. Even when he left—in a stolen car, the *idiot!*—he was still insisting he'd tell Miro about the baby and force him to give her up.

As if Miro would.

He wouldn't, would he—so close to the wedding? No,

never—not even if Alan told him everything. Miro would be disappointed in her—no, he'd be sorry for her, he'd smother her in the sympathy that Alan wasn't capable of. He would understand. Of course he would.

She was shivering now. But standing there in her underwear, bare feet on the stone flagged floor of the utility room, she *would* be shivering. It was natural. Except the whole country was suffering a heat wave; it was sweltering outside and not much cooler in here. Why was she shivering?

The hiss of water stopped, and the sound changed to a gentle sloshing as the machine started its Soak cycle. She could leave it now. The sound of slurping water was strangely soothing and for a moment, before going upstairs to put more clothes on, she pressed the palm of one hand against the front of the quivering machine. She was breathing shallowly—and the rap at the door came like an electric shock.

The door to outside was half glazed. Florian seemed framed in the window like a photograph, staring at her, a half smile on his broken face. He cocked his head to show that he wanted to come in.

Instinctively, her hand went to her breast. This was embarrassing. But she couldn't stay crouched like a startled teenager in the bath. She gestured him away, but he raised a hand and jiggled it in an opening movement. Could she open the door for him?

No, she mouthed, go away.

He shrugged, raised both palms, and stood there watching her. What should she do? If she left the room it would look as if she were running away from him, but she couldn't let him in—she was in her underclothes. These were especially frilly ones with lace. The bra was uplift. She couldn't let Florian into the small, intimate space of the utility room where he was bound to take the opportunity to stand close to her.

Beyond him through the glass she could see bright sunlight on the stable wall. If she talked to him out there, she thought, it would be no different to meeting him in her swimming costume beside a pool. Not that she'd want to. But at least in the open there'd be no threat.

She opened the door.

Florian didn't say anything. He didn't pretend not to gaze at her body. He didn't make a threatening move, he didn't move away, he merely stood waiting for her. She could smell him now—after all, he had been walking in the sun for about an hour.

She pushed past him and went into the middle of the cobbled courtyard. The heat hit her from all directions—from the sun above but also from the stable walls and the light grey cobbles. They were warm against her feet. The glass of the annex glinted at the end of the converted stable block. She asked what he wanted.

"Do you have the car key?"

Of course, he'd need the car to collect Miro.

"It's in the kitchen, in my handbag."

"Shall I come in?"

"I'll fetch it. You wait here."

He *was* sweating, she noticed, though he acted cool. She walked quickly through the utility room and on into the kitchen to where her handbag lay on the floor. Self-conscious in her bra and pants, she wondered whether to run upstairs and slip into another dress. But he might not wait outside. He might decide to come inside and see what was causing the delay. He might think she had invited him upstairs.

Ten minutes ago she had wanted him to appear. She had wanted him to help get rid of Alan.

She almost ran out with the key. For a moment she couldn't see him. He had moved out of the sunlight to lean

61

against the kitchen wall. He smiled at her in her under-clothes. "It *is* hot, isn't it?"

"Here's the key."

He reached out his hand but continued lounging against the wall. "That was a very long hot walk," he said. "My punishment. So . . . are we quits now?"

She frowned. Of course, they'd had an argument about the car. Hadn't she told him that she'd fire him? She couldn't remember. It seemed unimportant now. The business with Alan had pushed it from her mind. "Yes, yes," she muttered. "We'll forget it ever happened."

Florian jingled the keys. "So now we're friends."

She was calm again. With Miro home she felt safe and protected. He had come in hot and burdened with the afternoon's work and had quickly gone upstairs for his ritual shower. Before she'd known Miro, TV dramas had persuaded her that when well-off businessmen came home from work they went immediately to the cocktail cabinet—the 're-storative gin and tonic' being a natural part of middle-class life. But Miro didn't conform to conventional stereotypes. His habit—he was a man of habits—was to shoot upstairs, strip off his clothes and walk straight underneath a long hot shower. Much more healthy than gin and tonic.

Fully dressed now, Jo waited downstairs in their enormous living room. She sat back in a large settee, rubbing her hand lightly on its solid arm. Miro's fine house seemed a fortress. She had a powerful man upstairs and additional security, should it be necessary, from Florian in his quarters. None of which helped her when she answered the phone.

Alan said, "Hello, love. I was hoping to speak to your old man."

"He isn't here."

"Working late?"

"In a way."

"Doing overtime with his secretary?"

"What d'you want?"

"I mean, if you're on your own I could come over."

"Don't be stupid. What d'you want?"

"You didn't think I'd get your phone number, did you?"

"It's in the phone book."

"What time does he get in?"

"Late. He won't want to speak to you."

"Oh dear, and here's me going out later with the lads. Still, there's no hurry, is there? I can phone him any time this week."

"What do you hope to get out of this?"

"I'll see how he likes the truth."

Miro wouldn't be in the shower *every* time that Alan rang. He came out in fine good humour and Jo felt she responded shabbily, her thoughts skittish and her mind only half on what he said. They drank some wine and cuddled together in front of television. She thought of telling him, of giving her version before he heard Alan's on the phone, but she couldn't bring herself to do it. Despite what she'd told Alan, she knew Miro would be horrified to hear of her abortion. She was his innocent young darling. He knew there had been other men—boys, he'd call them, unimportant—but not a baby, an aborted child. He wanted that he and Joanna should have their own child—and after the mess and pain that had followed her abortion she didn't know if she was still capable of bearing one. She had never dared ask anyone.

She left Miro in the living room while she went to the kitchen to prepare a snack they could eat in front of television. With the kitchen lights on it looked dark outside.

Anyone could be out there: she'd never know. Someone could be watching her at this moment, as brightly lit as a picture on Miro's TV. But there was no one out there. This house was a mile from anywhere. She spread butter on some bread.

Why was Alan such a bastard? It had always been latent in him. If she were honest with herself, that hardness had been part of his appeal—most of his appeal, in truth. Two years in jail had done nothing to straighten him out. He had nursed his injuries and watched them fester.

What could she do about him? How could she stop him telling Miro? For one mad, ridiculous moment she thought of Miro's shotguns in their glass case. But that was madness. The only realistic solution—mad, illogical, but the only one she could think of—was to have someone put pressure on Alan and warn him off. Her throat was dry. She glanced at the dark window and licked her lips. There was no point hiding behind the evasive word 'someone'. She knew who she was thinking of—the one person who might be stronger than Alan, the one person who had offered help. But how could she turn to Florian? He'd do it, almost certainly. He'd do it to protect Miro, and he had already *told* her he'd do it for her. He had met Alan. He had warned her of the threat. But she hated Florian. She sighed, and changed knives to slice some cheese. Florian. No. She shivered. No.

Who else? How else?

The knife slid easily through the cheese. She suddenly realised she had sliced too much for two cheese sandwiches. It was only a snack—there was no need to overdo things. She looked at the mound of yellow slices on the plate. It didn't matter. They could afford it. A little wastage did no harm.

Florian, then. She reached for a tomato and cut into its soft wet flesh. Florian. She might hate the man, but she could conceal that. If she were civil to him he would serve her purpose.

Either later tonight or—no, not tonight—tomorrow morning, tomorrow morning before he took Miro to work, she would snatch a moment for a quiet talk with Florian, somewhere they could not be overheard, somewhere like his quarters perhaps—that lonely room he had across the courtyard in the annex.

Chapter 8

She phoned Dee at work. Early. Because Dee spent her days on the phone she didn't like to be telephoned—or her bosses didn't like her to be. A girl chatting into a mouthpiece should be generating business, not wasting company time on personal calls. But since Dee was on commission anyway, Jo said, her time must be her own affair? Dee said, no, tying up the line meant she was wasting company resources, and they'd say that if she wanted to deal with her own affairs she should vacate her seat and let someone else make money. Jo asked, what about the times when Dee came out of the office for shopping or to have her bridesmaid dress fitted or for—

"I'm not using the phone then, am I? D'you know what this is costing me?"

"Costing?"

"This is a selling opportunity. I lose commission when I talk to you."

"Well, I'm sorry if I—"

"How can I help you today?"

"Dee?"

"What d'you want—just at this moment?"

"Oh. Well, it's Alan again. You see—"

"Look, I'm sorry I gave him your address. Right? I told you."

"It's not that."

"What then?"

66

"I need *his* address now."

"I don't know. He's staying at his brother's, wherever that is."

"At Tommy's?"

"How many brothers does he have? I thought you never wanted to see him again?"

"I don't."

"So why are you calling?"

"At Tommy's place, you say?"

"I suppose he can't afford a place of his own."

"Not at the moment—"

"Will that be everything just now?"

She hadn't realised the main door to the annex would be locked. She had hoped to slip out the back of the main house, across the courtyard, into the conservatory and into the rear quarters without any chance of Miro spotting her. But she had to wait impatiently outside the locked glass door in the remorseless morning sunlight. She was about to turn away, leave it till later, when Florian appeared through the inner door and hurried across the plant-filled anteroom to open up.

"Something the matter?"

There was no trace of his usual supercilious sneer. He wore dark slacks and a white shirt unbuttoned at the neck. There was a dampness about his maimed face as if he had just washed.

She went straight inside. "I need to talk to you."

She ran straight along the short tiled path between the plants and through the unmarked inner door. A corridor lay parallel to the conservatory. She knew Florian's quarters would be along it to the left.

He came from the conservatory and closed the inner door. "Walk on in."

She hesitated, unsure which room to go into, but decided he wouldn't have meant the kitchenette because it was too small. She pushed an open door and stepped into Florian's bed-sitting room. It had a musky, almost feral smell overlaid with the deeper smell of coffee. The remains of a small breakfast lay on a low table, a television played silently and his bed had not yet been made. A tangled mound of sheets lay half on the floor.

"Would you like some coffee?" he asked.

"No, thank you."

She turned to face him. There was a chair but she didn't sit down. "I want your advice," she said. Advice sounded better than help.

"Advice," he repeated wonderingly.

"We don't have much time."

"True," he laughed. "I'm taking Miro to work soon, but perhaps—"

"You know we're getting married next week."

He waited.

"Well, I've run into a bit of a problem."

He continued to wait. She said, "I didn't think this would happen, but . . ."

She stared at him. He asked, "Didn't think what would happen?"

"You warned me."

His face cleared. "The young man?"

She nodded.

Florian thought for a moment, then became businesslike. "Is he a past or present boyfriend?"

It was a relief that Florian had come straight to the point. "Past."

"Excuse me while I finish dressing." He smiled and picked up his tie from the back of a chair. "Do you really want my advice or do you want me to do something?"

"Either."

Florian was knotting the tie. "Is he blackmailing you?"

"No."

"Then what?"

"He wants to stop the marriage."

Florian glanced at his tie in the mirror. "Unless you do what?"

"Nothing."

"He just wants to stop the marriage?"

She had to press on. "Miro says he can rely on you to take care of things—all sorts of things—not just drive the car. I mean . . . I don't know if you can help me."

He nodded, walking across the room to fetch his jacket. She said, "Alan phoned me here last night. And he came to the house yesterday afternoon."

"Ah." Florian shrugged into his jacket. "I should have walked home faster."

"You weren't to know."

He stood ready for work. She repeated, "Miro says he relies on you for all sorts of things. He says you do a lot more for him than just drive the car—whatever that means."

Florian seemed guarded. He drew his cheeks in before he spoke. "I do look after the flowers in the conservatory."

"More than that."

"And I prune the roses and cut the lawn."

"No, I—"

"But I'm a poor gardener."

She said, "Florian, I don't know what to do."

He said, "Miro treats me as an equal but we both know he's the boss. No doubt about that. We're at the stage where he doesn't have to tell me what to do—I anticipate his needs. More like a butler, if you like." Florian caught her eye. "I was nobody when I got this job. I owe him a lot." He paused. "Before you came, Miro and I ate together at times. He always treated me well."

Her mouth was dry. "Well, I shall try to do the same, Florian. D'you think you can help me with this . . . problem?"

He nodded. "Leave it to me."

He adjusted his tie, as if he'd said all he needed to. But she made eye contact. "What exactly will you do?"

"You want details?" She looked away, and he smiled. "Truth is, I don't know yet. What does he have on you?"

She shook her head.

"Does he have evidence? Letters? Pictures?"

"I don't think so."

"He'd have told you. So there's nothing you want me to get back from him?"

"I don't think so."

"Why are you afraid of him?"

"I . . . don't want to say."

Florian exhaled. "We all have our secrets."

She said carefully, "If you do . . . manage to stop him, I'll be really grateful."

"Of course."

"I don't know how I can pay you back."

"Don't worry about it."

She held his gaze questioningly. "I don't have much money . . ."

He snorted. "Money!"

"Though when I'm married I suppose I will—"

He shook his head, his gaze never leaving her. "Don't mention money again."

"I'll be in your debt."

He studied her. "Are we reconciled now?"

"Reconciled? Ye-es."

"Are we agreed that I should act for you?"

She nodded.

"I'd like to hear you say it, Jo."

She flinched at his using her name, as if it were the first time that he'd used it. But she'd have to get used to it, she realised. She licked her lips and said, "All right. I want you to act for me as you think best. If you stop him, I'll be truly grateful."

Florian raised a finger to his scar. He wasn't hiding it from her today. "It's good to hear your soft words, Jo—even if I know you don't really mean them! Will you write down his address for me?"

He handed her his notebook, and without thinking she began writing on the open page. He watched eagerly. She said, "That's his brother's address. Tommy. I don't know if Tommy's got a job or whether he's in or not. They might both be there."

"Anything special I should say to him?"

She sighed. "Do I have to think of . . . everything?"

He turned to a fresh page in his notebook. "Write him a note, saying you need to meet him urgently, and I'm to fetch him in the car. Don't worry, it's just in case."

She sighed, then wrote the brief note. Looking up, she said, "I wish I were a man."

"Don't say that!" he laughed.

"Then I could do it myself."

He raised his eyebrows. "Let me be the man for you."

She let out her breath. "Alan can be dangerous."

"Good. Because a dangerous service deserves a precious reward."

A bolt of anger flared in her eyes. "I said I'll pay you. Somehow."

"I don't want money."

She waved a hand and shrugged. "Something."

He leant forward. "Something precious?"

"Whatever," she said dismissively.

He smiled. "That's fine."

Jo sat back sharply, to break any intimacy that Florian might have thought they had. "Can you do this?" she asked briskly.

He turned to the mirror and gave a nod. "You'll see no more of him."

She looked away. "Be careful," she whispered.

"I'll be careful for both of us."

She shivered.

Chapter 9

Florian had parked the Lexus outside a small line of shops on the main Cricklade Road. He wouldn't take it into the Penhill Estate—they'd think a satellite had fallen to earth. In Penhill it wasn't wise to flaunt your money, nor was it the easiest place to watch someone's house. He walked up and down the drab residential street, and asked himself why he didn't march to their door and get it done. The worst that could happen was that Alan's brother Tommy would answer the door. Not that Florian cared about an out-of-work Swindon oik, but the fewer people who saw him the better. Preferably no one but Alan. If Tommy was in, Florian could ask for Alan, and if Tommy was there on his own Florian could smile pleasantly and disappear. But if they were both in, Alan was bound to recognise him and tell his brother who he was. Then both brothers would be involved.

On his third circuit Florian noticed some kids keeping an eye on him. They lived here; he didn't. He could walk *through* the area, he could walk to someone's house, but he couldn't wander about. No one did. Glancing down a side road leading back to the main road he saw the perspex dome of a phone box. Of course, he thought. Get your brain working.

Any phone directory had long since vanished from the phone box, so Florian phoned Directory Enquiries. "Thomas Pirie," he said, giving the address. Presumably the boy *had* a

73

phone. He'd not be ex-directory.

The number was recited back to him electronically.

Florian thanked the machine. Thank you, God.

When he rang the number no one answered. No one in or no one up? Well, it *was* only lunchtime. They were out. They had to be. Florian pursed his lips. What if Tommy and Alan came home together? As they probably would.

Florian leant against the curved dome of the phone box. Wouldn't it be better to get Joanna involved? She could call Alan any time and ask him to meet her—and then let him find Florian waiting instead. Much more sensible—and it would guarantee a meeting with Alan on his own. Plus it kept Joanna involved. She had to be a part of this—which was why he had asked her to write in his notebook. Florian didn't know what, if anything, he could do with it but the evidence might come in useful.

Back at his flat in the annex she had all but acknowledged the change in their relationship—all those weeks freezing him out and now she needed him. Because she was scared of this boy. If Florian could remove the threat she'd be in his debt. She had acknowledged that. She thought he meant money but Florian could feel her in his arms already, her fingers in his hair, her breath on his cheek, her voice whispering how she had learned to love his crooked face.

She had been eating a light lunch beneath the old mulberry tree, its drooping canopy of large, floppy leaves forming a cool shelter from the heat. There was a thin haze high in the sky, and though the sun was less scorching than it had been, the weather seemed more oppressive. Birds had stopped calling to each other. Even the flies flew heavy with heat. Out in the wilting flower beds a cloud of summer butterflies flitted unaffected from bloom to bloom.

Florian parted the branches and stepped into the gloomy shade. Trapped by the branches, the air felt heavy and close as if it had lain undisturbed for several days. Jo wore a red sun frock. Her black hair was hanging loose.

"What did you say to him?"

"He wasn't in."

She looked irritated, as he knew she would. She said, "He'll call round to the house again—I know he will. He'll either come or he'll phone Miro."

"Not yet. He hasn't given you enough time."

"Alan doesn't care. He's determined to stop the wedding."

"Why?" Florian fingered a mulberry branch. The berries were hard and still green.

"It doesn't matter," she said.

"It matters to him."

She tossed her head. "This was a waste of time. I thought I could rely on you."

"I can't talk to him if he isn't there."

"*Talk* to him!"

"What did you *want* me to do?"

She stared at him. Dappled light made her olive skin look mottled. "Stop him," she said. The heavy air seemed to sap her energy, but she managed to add, "He'll come round again tonight."

"No."

"I know he will."

Florian kept hold of the branch. It gave his hands something to do and it helped him hold back from her. "I'll scare him off."

She sneered. "You haven't even seen him."

"Not yet. It would be faster if you called him—"

"No chance!"

75

"Why are you frightened?"

"Why d'you think?"

"I don't think."

They stared blankly at each other. She was moist with sweat. She hated the air so dead and hot. Then she said, "He's just going to wreck my life, that's all."

Suddenly, Florian stepped away through the curtain of leaves back onto the lawn. He couldn't trust himself in the enclosed space with her, and he preferred the sun to that fetid gloom—though the sun was lost now behind thin cloud. The air shimmered. He said, "I don't see what he has on you. Miro won't be interested that you once had a boyfriend."

"He's vicious."

"So?"

Through the branches he watched her, seated at the table. She looked wretched. In a small voice she asked, "Won't you help me—please?"

He smiled to himself. "Tell me what he has on you."

Jo sighed. Then she took a sharp breath as if she had decided to explain. "He's been in prison."

"Surprise."

"He's only just come out. And he wants to carry on where he left off. But he's been away two years. That's a long time—another life."

Florian waited but she did not continue. He asked, "Have you been with him since you've been going out with Miro?"

"God, no."

"Then where's the problem? He's just a nuisance."

"You don't know what he's like."

"To me he seemed a punk. But obviously you haven't told me everything." He waited. "Perhaps we should forget the whole idea."

He moved away.

"No, wait. There is something more."

That was easy, he thought, stepping back through the branches. "Tell me."

She looked so young and vulnerable that Florian had to clutch again at a protective branch. She said, "Before Alan went to jail he . . . well, he raped me. More than once. He tried to make me . . . his sex slave."

Florian didn't believe that. "Oh, really? Tell me more."

Her eyes flashed. "Why—d'you want to get off on the details?"

"I need to understand—"

"You don't *need* the details."

He smiled faintly. "I need more than you've told me."

"Forget it."

"All right, I've forgotten it."

She glared at him. He said, "Come on. I don't believe a word of this, Joanna. I think you and this boy have been lovers and now you want rid of him. Simple as that."

"You're wrong."

He shrugged. "It isn't a problem, Jo. If you want him sorted, fine—but please don't tell me lies." He let go of the branch and moved to the table and placed both hands on it, opposite where she sat. "Don't play me for a fool."

She stared at his hands, capable and strong on the little garden table. "There is something else," she said. "Before he . . . went inside we . . . got engaged."

"The truth at last. You didn't marry him?"

"God, no!"

"So what's the problem? You're allowed to change your mind."

"But what would Miro think? Alan still has the engagement ring I bought him."

"Big deal."

"It's engraved from me to him."

"So?"

She looked down. "You're not going to help me, are you?"

He paused. "Is that the whole story?"

He watched her but she would not look up at him. He shrugged. "So. You want me to remove this guilty secret?"

He continued watching her. There was no sound in the sheltered garden. Even the birds were silent. Finally, she looked up at him. "I do."

Chapter 10

Dee had backcombed and sprayed her hair so hard that it stood right away from her head. She looked as if she had been electrocuted, brought back to life like Frankenstein's bride. But if she had the bride's bright staring eyes, her flesh was alive, her blood was warm and her breath blew sweet across succulent red lips. Jasper sat opposite her in the restaurant and tried to keep his thoughts on the menu. He had tasted nothing yet.

"Mind if I remove my jacket?"

Dee shrugged prettily, so Jasper eased out of his jacket and draped it across a spare chair. He was sweating slightly.

She said, "You'd think this place would have air con."

To help against the weather the restaurant had installed several electric fans, but their breeze was warm, balmy, as on a tropical beach. Jasper wiped his pink neck.

"Too hot for you?" she asked.

"A drink will cool us down."

"Drink makes me hot."

"Then we'll order two bottles," he laughed, loosening his tie. "Heat gives *me* the itch."

"The itch for what?"

He chuckled. "What do *you* think?"

Dee fanned herself with the large glossy menu. Without his jacket Jasper still managed to look dapper. He was dark haired, trim and had an attractive evening shadow—the kind of man who ought to shave twice a day. He said, "It must be my hot blood."

"Let's hope."

Dee glanced at the menu.

"You know what medicine I need for this itch?"

"I can't guess."

"Two ingredients com*pounded* together that will tame the maddest blood in town."

"Well, fancy."

Jasper shot the cuffs of his expensive white shirt. "But of course this medicine must be properly stirred."

She met his eye. "And I suppose you've got just the spoon for it?"

"More of a paddle, I'd say."

She giggled. "You need a drink."

"And a special vessel to drink from."

She offered a wine glass. He leant forward. "That's not what I had in mind."

Their heads touched. But raising her glass was a call to the wine waiter. As the man scurried over, Dee and Jasper looked like naughty children caught out late. They peeped at each other furtively as Jasper studied the choices. "Something white?"

"Sounds too light."

Their lips twitched at a private joke they could not have explained. "Something wild," Jasper said.

She knew he was married. She didn't know what he did for Miro—*with* Miro, as he had put it—but he was a junior partner, a chartered surveyor, one of Miro's oldest friends. She wasn't sure whether this was a good thing or not. If anything came of tonight—and let's face it, she thought, something probably would—in years to come they could find themselves facing each other across Miro's dining table, Jasper with his unsuspecting wife, and she herself with a rich future husband. Would it matter? Certainly *she* wouldn't care: Jasper wouldn't be the only old flame she'd seen flickering in another girl's hearth.

Jo couldn't relax. She was afraid that Alan might phone. To avoid the call she had asked Miro if they could eat out in the garden—the hot weather wouldn't last, she pretended.

"I thought you hated the heat?"

This was in the front garden, near the Three Graces fountain, where spray from the water drifted against them through the warm air. The sun was low in the sky and the horizon had turned an ominous pale mauve.

"We'll have a picnic," Miro said. He had been in a restless mood all day, having chosen not to go with his clients on that morning's shoot. Jo wondered if he blamed her for missing it—but it was his decision. He could have gone if he'd wanted. But an open air picnic tonight might cheer him up.

They spread a blanket on the dry lawn with a bottle of white wine, a French loaf, some fruit and lots of cheese. Miro had olives. At first he had suggested they set a table in the enclosed courtyard between the main house and the stable block, but Jo said it would be too shady there. She wanted to eat out on the lawn. Where they wouldn't hear the phone.

There were insects in the evening air, lingering in the heat and attracted by mist from the fountain.

Joanna said, "It's gorgeous here."

"Apart from the midges."

"The house, miles from anywhere. So peaceful."

"You're not bored?"

"I like the quiet."

"We're not that distant. Barely a mile from the village."

In an earlier century Electra Court—then called Penrose House—had been the manor for the nearby tiny village, but the houses there had long ceased to be farm cottages and the little church now shared its minister with several other small hamlets. Once that church too had belonged to the manor.

Miro poured two glasses of wine and replaced the bottle in the cool fountain. "Sometimes I worry that you won't always like it here, far from everywhere."

"This is bliss."

But she wasn't feeling blissful. While she sat with Miro in the garden, Florian and Alan might be having their assignation. She tried to imagine what they'd say. Alan was not an easy man, and despite Florian's confidence, she didn't see how he could warn Alan off. Even if he forced him to *agree* to leave her alone, there was no guarantee that Alan would keep his word. He only had to pick up the phone.

Miro said, "Perhaps you'll go out to work again."

"In your office?"

"Somewhere else, where you wouldn't feel you were always under observation. Perhaps voluntary work—it wouldn't matter what it paid, but you do need an occupation, Jo. Once we're married you won't want to hang around here day after day."

Married. Less than a week till they'd have the Blessing in the little village church—but with Alan's threat hanging over her, these next few days might seem a lifetime.

"I don't think I'm cut out to be Lady Bountiful."

Miro gazed at her. The evening was still light but now that the sun was below the trees there were no shadows on the lawn. "You're not . . . wondering?"

"Second thoughts? No." She stared past him. "Look at the colour of the sky. Dirty yellow."

Miro turned to glance at it. "The air feels heavy. Time for the weather to break."

"I've been waiting for days."

Florian sat in the Lexus in the Moonrakers car park. The pub looked like a roadhouse, but had long since been swallowed by Swindon suburbs. On its prominent and well-lit corner site the pub was renowned for its female clientele. They felt safe there. They'd come singly, or in pairs or gangs for a rowdy night out. There were nights that sensible men avoided—older women nights, when they painted their tired faces, strained into tight clothes and marched into the Moonrakers to take over the world. There were more and more older women, he thought—or perhaps they went out more nowadays. They got raucous with drink, and the Moonrakers was known to local lads as an easy place for a pick-up, if you weren't choosy. To Florian it seemed a strange idea, to go to a place where men were looked over and picked out by women—it shouldn't be like that. Men should call the shots. Florian was old fashioned, a throwback to the previous millennium where men whistled and women blushed. He sat outside in the Moonrakers car park, disinclined to go in and be inspected like meat. Even here, in the warm heavy twilight, occasional women had spotted him sitting alone in the expensive car. Some had nodded and grinned at him. One group had laughed. A blonde girl on her own had paused, held his gaze, then slipped shyly inside the pub. On another night . . .

Alan would know the Moonrakers. Florian had told Jo to write the note asking him to meet her there, to come alone, and Alan would read a promise into that. But he was taking his time. Waiting in the car, Florian realised how women must feel—stared at and appraised, eyed up and turned down, kept waiting. That's what Alan was doing—keeping him waiting for a date. Keeping *her* waiting is what he thought. Assuming that he *was* coming, of course. Florian gritted his teeth. He felt even more like a woman—you arrive first, you're kept waiting, and you begin to wonder if the man will turn up.

Twenty minutes.

Florian saw Alan before he turned into the car park—on foot, of course: the punk couldn't afford a car and he *wouldn't* afford a taxi. Florian was out of his car before Alan came in. Alan didn't see him at first and he paused a moment to pat down his sandy hair. If he had worn a tie he'd have straightened it.

Then he saw Florian, with the Lexus behind.

Florian said, "You got her note?"

"How did *you* know?"

"She asked me to collect you."

Alan frowned. "She said we'd be meeting here."

"She's found somewhere more romantic."

Alan stared at him. Florian didn't smile. He didn't have to look persuasive. "I'm to drop you off, leave you alone together, and pick you up later—that's what she said."

Alan paused. "You really her chauffeur?"

"It's a job."

Alan sniffed. "She's come up in the world."

"You only live once." Florian looked at him. "So make the most of it."

Alan lolled in the back of the Lexus and ran his rough hand along the leather. "I could get used to this."

"You wish."

"She got money now, or is everything his?"

"Oh, once they're married, you know."

"Fifty-fifty?"

Florian glanced once in his rear mirror. "Jo's the sort of girl you should be nice to."

"Yeah, I'll be nice to her. Where are we going?"

They were leaving Swindon, on the main road towards the Cotswolds. "A surprise."

"I don't like surprises."

"You'll like this."

In the orange twilight as they swooped down Blunsden Hill the wide green valley looked flat and tired. On the far horizon the Cotswold hills were blue ripples in the landscape and the church tower at Cricklade stood erect from the valley floor. You could imagine the whole valley flooded, leaving just that tower above the water—a vast expanse of water and a single tower above the surface like Excalibur. There was a dull greyness in the air but the car's air conditioning hid how stifling it was outside. Florian flicked on the side lights. It was the first time he'd used them for months.

Alan said, "Hope we're going to a pub. I haven't eaten yet."

Florian smiled to himself. Save your money.

"This isn't the way."

In the back of the Lexus, Alan stirred. For the last five minutes neither of them had said anything, Florian's monosyllabic answers discouraging conversation. Alan didn't like small talk anyway. But they were past Cricklade now, the wide straight road cutting imperiously through the fields. Florian told him they'd soon be turning off.

"We've gone too far for Jo's house," Alan grumbled. "I've been there. I should know."

"I *live* there."

"We didn't ought to have come past Cricklade."

"We're not going to the house."

He was slowing as they approached the exit for the Cotswold Water Park.

Alan said, "I thought we was—"

"No, she doesn't want you to meet Miro."

Alan grunted. "What sort of name is that?"

Florian turned left. Between the pretty villages here— South Cerney, Cerney Wick, Ashton Keynes and Somerford Keynes—the old gravel pits had been flooded and converted into lakes. Some were used for boating, some for fishing, and some had been naturalised. Some were busy, some were not. Some were accessible, some were isolated. In the evenings most were isolated.

Alan asked, "Where are we going out here?"

"Somewhere quaint."

"What's that mean?"

Florian didn't reply. He'd prefer Alan not to get agitated but if he did it was too bad. He couldn't go anywhere. He couldn't do anything in the back. Florian drove the car swiftly past the first more popular lakes, deeper into the park. It was hardly park-like at all, he thought—in parts you could drive straight down the quiet lanes and think you were on an ordinary country drive. Only some of the lakes were signposted, but Florian knew the one he wanted.

He turned up a track. Not signposted.

It was a dirt track, rutted and sandy, sprinkled with gravel from old pits. Dull green bushes edged the path and the car's immaculate suspension couldn't hide the unevenness of the track. Stones clunked beneath the chassis.

"We're never meeting her here," Alan said.

Florian smiled. "It isn't how it looks."

"Is this a set-up?"

"She wants somewhere private. You're her guilty secret, aren't you?"

Florian watched him in the mirror. Alan was alert now—upright in his seat, jaw set, fists clenched, eyes darting.

Florian stopped the car.

When he got out and moved to the rear door, Alan stayed inside. Florian opened the door. Alan glared up at him, but Florian smiled encouragingly. "Coming?"

Alan was panting slightly, as if shocked by the warm breeze rushing into the car, displacing the cool of the air-conditioner. The turbid evening air lay almost visible outside. There wasn't a sound.

They stared at each other. Florian said, "All right, I'll tell you—although she told me not to say anything. She fancies a romantic tryst down by the waterside. Come on."

He stepped back two paces. Alan climbed out of the car. Florian looked relaxed and unthreatening.

He said, "Joanna's waiting for you."

She had undone the top two buttons of her shirt—partly because the evening was so close and partly because she could tell he wanted sex. The limp shirt lay lifeless against her olive skin and a faint sheen of sweat clung to the white V of her neck bone where it pressed beneath the flesh. Jo had pulled the shirt from her waistband and it flapped against her hips as she and Miro strolled hand in hand beside the rose bed. The wine and hot weather had relaxed him and he kept nudging her as they walked, holding her hand against his thigh. They were both barefoot, and in the air hung the scent of roses and Madonna lilies. The grass beneath their feet was hard, parched of water, and each leaf of the bushes looked crisp and curled.

From a nearby tree a blackbird trilled. But it was too hot and the bird gave up. The sky was losing colour, becoming muted, dirty white—but the air was warm now and didn't need the sun. There was not the faintest breeze and it was as if Miro and Jo were breathing the same air over and over again, sucking out its oxygen, depleting it, until eventually there would be none left to keep them awake.

Miro stopped. Their bodies were so close that she stopped in the same step. They stood on his hardened lawn as he turned to her for a kiss. They were warm, breathless, with moisture in their mouths. She felt his hand run through her hair. His fingers stroked her neck. His hand slid gently across her shoulder and ran slowly down her front. She wasn't wearing a bra. He squeezed her breast softly, rubbed his thumb across her nipple, then moved his hand up beneath her arm where she was ticklish—but he didn't tickle, he only stroked her, and she shivered in his arms. He ran his hand down her side and as his fingers rippled across her ribs she trembled again. This was the nicest part. The prelude to sex was more enjoyable than the act itself. The cosseting of his hands. His warm lips. Miro moved his hand across the front of her thigh, pausing a moment at the little bone which jutted out. He stroked through two layers of material and she wondered what he could feel. There was nothing there—a woman had nothing—and through the material he would only feel her empty thigh, while a man had hardness, his trousers packed. She ran her own hands down to his buttocks—he liked that, Jo knew—then slid one hand round to stroke him at the front. The hardness, coiled so tight. He could have had a kitten in there—she felt it stir. He was tugging at her shirt buttons—one hand inside her shirt, impatient, unwilling to wait till every button was undone, pushing roughly against her breast. She felt his other hand at her waistband, fumbling to find how the skirt released. But they were too tight against each other, her hand on his behind, pulling his body close, and when he forced his hand inside the waistband she squirmed sideways. "Not out here."

"No one can see."

He pressed his lips against her mouth.

"Not here," she said.

"Lie down."

"The ground's too hard—"

He changed grip and suddenly picked her up and carried her across the lawn. He said, "Under the mulberry tree."

She laughed, nervously. "It's horrible there. Too hard."

She was panicking in his arms. She had to think straight. Sex was nice, wasn't it? Maybe it wasn't earth-shattering, like in the movies, but perhaps tonight she could make it so. It was only fair to him. "All right—but not under the tree."

"Out here."

He plopped her down. She clutched at him to find her feet. Her thoughts were with Alan and Florian—and she didn't want to think of them. She wanted to think of Miro, to be good to him, to satisfy his need. She must be especially passionate with him—she must drive those other thoughts away and give her man what he deserved. He was a good man, her saviour.

He pulled her skirt down. She was clad in only the open shirt. She reached up to cup his head, grabbed his wiry hair and pulled him closer into a kiss. He clasped her wriggling body, crushing her, and she squeezed her hands between their chests and began fiddling with his shirt buttons. She knew he wanted her. Now.

"Let me," she said. "Let me undress you."

He released her. While she quickly undid his shirt Miro stamped on the grass as if the ground were roasting hot. Then she started on his trousers, pulling down the zip, unclipping the waistband, pulling the trousers down together with his undershorts. He seemed more patient now. His fingers were in her hair. He pulled away from her and for a moment she was left kneeling on the prickly grass, hands stretched out as if in prayer. He was naked apart from his socks, while she still wore her flimsy shirt. He reached down to her, but she rolled away laughing, so he dropped to his knees and chased her on the ground. Jo sprang up and ran across the lawn.

"It's too hot," she called. "Follow me!"

As Miro clambered to his feet Jo ran to the rippling Three Graces fountain, where she waited, one hand in the cool water, watching as Miro sprinted across the lawn. She lifted one leg and stepped into the bowl. The water was cold, not cool, but she found it heavenly to be in the cold after so much awful heat. She stood beneath the fountain and let it dribble down her shirt.

Miro arrived and gazed at her as if the statue had come to life, then he pulled off his socks and clambered into the chilly water. He shuddered and took her in his arms.

"This is life!" he called. Water all down their faces. Bodies soaking wet. Her shirt a sodden rag. He pulled it from her, and she heard it plop somewhere behind her in the bowl.

They slithered against each other in the falling water, their feet splashing. His hand dropped, her legs parted, and like a frog slipping beneath a lily leaf Miro entered his bride to be.

Alan hesitated by the bushes. It was still light, he could see water through them, but the chances of Jo being there looked slim. Florian pushed on through a gap in the bushes and called back to him: "Come on. This is it."

His voice was normal. He wasn't trying to be quiet. Alan parted the branches and came through. They were on a gravel bank three feet above the lake. Florian began to pick his way down to it. "This is a narrow descent," he said. "Let me help you."

"I'm not a kid," Alan snarled.

There wasn't a path but it was not difficult to reach the water. He kept his eye on Florian as he joined him. "She ain't here, is she?"

Alan's hands dangled. He was ready for him.

Florian smiled disarmingly. "I told you—she wants it to be like in a book."

The sky was darkening but they could see each other clearly. Florian was relaxed. He looked out across the lapping water and said, "She comes here with Miro sometimes. He has a boat."

"She *is* here, then?"

"Rely on it. Well, my job's finished now. I was only asked to deliver you."

Alan sniffed. "Thanks," he grunted. "Kind of you."

"My pleasure. I'll leave you now. Look out across the lake. You'll see something you never dreamt that you'd see."

Alan clenched his fists. "Like what?"

Florian pointed across the lake. "Feast your eyes on that. Keep your eye straight. See that tall tree the other side?"

Alan flicked a glance but returned his gaze to Florian. "What is this?"

"You know the Greek legends, Alan?"

It was the first time that Florian had used his name. This was getting weird. "What?"

"Echo and Narcissus—remember?"

Florian was grinning at him like a pedantic schoolteacher.

"I've had enough of this," Alan said. Somewhere across the water he heard a gull shriek.

"Jo told me the story," Florian said. "Narcissus—that's the man, of course—was so wrapped up in himself he didn't realise that the beautiful Echo—that's the girl—had been passionately in love with him all the while. Though she would call to him, he wouldn't answer."

"You think I've time for this?"

"That's what *she* said: you won't listen. You just won't listen."

They stared at each other. The only sound was cold water lapping at the shore. A faint breeze came off the lake. There hadn't been a breeze for days. The gull shrieked again.

Florian said, "Echo followed Narcissus about, to see what he did with himself every day."

"For Christ's sake."

"And one day she followed him to a lake." Their eyes met. "Guess what Echo saw?"

Alan grunted.

"It was probably a lakeside just like this. Think of it: calm evening, no one about, just two people and all that clear water."

"This is one of them stories where they kill each other, right?"

Florian chuckled. "This is a *romantic* story. Jo wants tonight to be special for you."

"What, this Echo bird kills him? Gets her fucking servant to kill him? What's the plot?"

Florian shook his head. "Her *fucking* servant? I like that, I really like that, Alan. Her fucking servant. No, it's a pity you never read the classics."

"I'm outa here."

"You're walking out on her?"

"It's a set up. She ain't here."

"Alan, she doesn't want tonight to be ordinary. This story has been retold for two thousand years."

The wind stirred the leaves. It wasn't a cold wind. It was as if a Greek God had sighed.

"Echo saw Narcissus at the lake. And you know what he

was doing, don't you, Alan? Everyone knows that."

"Yeah? Well, I don't. So what?"

"Narcissus thought he was alone. He did what he always did when he was alone."

"Played with himself?"

"In a way. He knelt down at the water's edge and peered into the water. Guess what he saw? The most beautiful face in the world."

"*His* face, weren't it?"

"That's the point. That's why Narcissus is famous. He couldn't stop staring at his own reflection."

"What's this got to do with me?"

"The next bit. Echo comes up behind him—"

"Yeah?" asked Alan warily.

"And appears behind his shoulder. Suddenly there are *two* beautiful faces in the water." Florian paused. "You know what Jo is like. Imagine just two beautiful people in this lovely spot together. Romantic? I'll say."

"She thought of this?"

"It's a fantasy. You know. Your face in the water. Suddenly her reflection appears beside you. You gaze at each other in the water."

"Yeah, but *you'd* be here."

"My job is done."

"Bollocks."

Again the gull shrieked. Florian said, "Trust me. I'm going. Now, you kneel down by the water—"

"Oh no—"

"Ssh. She'll hear you."

"She's not here, for fuck's sake."

"Echo comes to the waterside. She's naked."

"Jo—naked? You're kidding me."

"Echo is a nymph. She comes naked."

"You saying Jo's here?"

"You know the story. Echo is naked, hiding in the bushes, waiting for the appearance of the only man she loves—that's the kind of thing a girl gets off on, isn't it?"

Alan looked at him, wondering. Florian's scar seemed to glow as he said, "I'll fetch her for you. But do the girl a favour. Do what she wants."

"Like what?"

"Play along with it. Be Narcissus. Kneel down, look at your reflection in the water—"

"Come on!"

"Seriously. In this light, the sun fading, you can see yourself clearly in the water. Look in the water, Alan. Try it."

Alan hesitated. He shook his head slightly. He didn't know what the hell was going on. He glanced at the water. "I don't see nothing."

"No, get down to it. I'll show you."

Florian dropped to his knees by the water. "Yes, that's it. Like a mirror." He looked up at Alan, six feet away from him. "Look into the water with me."

Alan licked his lips. He stepped nearer the lakeside, then stopped. "This is stupid."

Florian eased back onto his haunches. "You think I'm going to push you in—get your clothes wet?"

Alan looked uncomfortable. Florian said dreamily, "Let Echo come to you."

Alan shook his head again. Florian said, "Don't spoil the moment." He stood up. "I shall bring her, leave her, and come back again in an hour." He moved into the bushes. "Kneel down and wait for her. Look at your reflection."

Florian disappeared. Alan glanced about. It was still light but the sky had dulled. The surface of the water looked heavy as lead. He could hear the warm breeze in the bushes, and though he felt it on his face the air felt as heavy as the water. All across the empty lake little wavelets rippled and swelled, but when Alan glanced down in the shallows the surface shone.

He knelt down.

Alan glanced behind him, then peered briefly in the water. He looked behind him again. Nothing. No one. Even the gull had disappeared. But Alan had seen his reflection in the water. What of that? He glanced again and looked up. He had seen his face, a blur in the slurping water, and he'd had a vision of how it might be—another face behind him, Jo at his shoulder, naked like the nymph. Perhaps that was what she wanted. The night was warm. He bent forward, leant out across the water and yes, he could see his face peering back at him from the water. The reflection moved. It was like seeing himself in a film. He saw his mouth slightly open, his sandy hair flopping loose, his own eyes, his familiar reflection, himself in reverse, his cautious smile. Any moment the nymph would come.

He heard her. He saw a grinning face in the rippling water. It wasn't her face—

Florian grabbed his hair, pulled his head back, rammed his knee into his spine. A knife at Alan's throat. Now he pushed his head forwards, towards the water. Alan grabbed at Florian's hand. But too late. Florian carved across his throat and oh, the knife was sharp! It hardly hurt. Alan *saw* the pain before he felt it. Florian held his head above the water and Alan saw the line of red, saw it widen, saw his own flesh curl apart—the blood spurting, the great vomit of dark red fluid splashing down into the water across the image of his face.

Suddenly he could see nothing. He heard a roar and Florian's voice: "You fool! You thought she'd come to you? You can wait till the end of time."

Florian felt him sag, a dead weight. He extended his arm and held Alan by the hair, out across the water, heaving back on Alan's head to make the great gash widen across his throat, and the gaping edges tear apart, and the last blobs of blood and mucous plop like pebbles into the lake.

Then he let go of Alan's hair and the body collapsed into the shallows—chest in the water, head half submerged, a pool of darkness swilling out from it and away. Florian sat back and listened. Not a sound—until once again, like a returning fury, the gull swooped across the darkened lake and called harshly, its cry strident in the air. Another gull appeared, then another. A small flock of gulls followed across the water, shrieking as they flew, their noise beating against the wavelets. A surge, and they disappeared.

Suddenly it was quiet again.

The water around Alan's head was clearing. Every drop of spilt blood had fallen into the water and on the dry gravel shore were no obvious marks of scuffle. If Alan could have been pushed off and floated into the lake no one would have known they had been there. But it wasn't as easy as that.

There were clouds in the sky. They shook the moonlight so it lay dappled, as if through leaves. When Florian looked down at Alan's body the light made a tiny glint on his hand. What's this that sparkles? He saw a ring, Jo's ring, the one she'd told him she had given Alan when they engaged. The ring she had foolishly had engraved. It might be worth nothing, Florian thought, but it would serve to prove his work. He took Alan's hand and tried to slide the ring free. But it was tight. He dragged Alan's surprisingly heavy arm across so he could dangle his fingers in the water and try again on wetted flesh. But the ring wouldn't move. Stuck fast. Even in death it wouldn't part.

Florian tried to prise it off with his knife but though he cut into the flesh the ring would not slide past Alan's knuckle. He began hacking at the finger. But the bone seemed made of iron. He carved into the space between the fingers, cutting through sinew and tendon along Alan's hand until suddenly his knife slid more easily, up the hand, along—then stuck again. Florian pulled at the finger, snapped the joint and ripped it from the hand as he might tug a chicken's leg from a roast. He heaved at it, helped it with the knife, until it was finally hacked away.

He looked at the finger in his hand. The ring seemed to have sunk into its flesh. Florian couldn't be bothered to pick at the ring to work it free, so he reached into his pocket, took out a handkerchief, then put the hankie on the ground and dipped the finger in lake water to wash off the blood. There was little red blood left inside it. He swished it around. When it seemed clean, Florian wrapped the finger tightly in his handkerchief and placed it carefully in his pocket. Then he looked at the body and stood up.

He knew what he must do next.

Miro sat in the fountain like an overgrown child in his bath, washing himself with imaginary soap. Jo stepped out onto the lawn and looked at the darkening sky. The air was warm but the sun had disappeared behind dense clouds. She felt like a goddess, naked on the lawn, comfortable in the warm air. Miro chatted in his bath.

She was hardly listening. Her thoughts were with Florian—would Alan listen to what he said? Despite the humid atmosphere, she shivered, while Miro stood in the water, chattering after sex. "Definitely looks like rain."

"We've nothing to dry ourselves on."

They grinned at each other, faintly ridiculous in their damp nakedness, then began gathering their scattered clothes. Miro had plenty to grin about, she thought. He'd had outdoor sex, had proved his masculinity again, and had found a new game to play in his precious fountain. He'd want to play that game again. He said, "It *is* raining. I felt a splatter then."

Jo held out her hand, though being naked she could feel the drops all over her skin.

Miro trailed after Jo towards the house. Rain was falling harder, but he remained as indifferent to the rain as when he had been sporting in the fountain. A clap of thunder struck. Miro began to run. Jo waited under the mock Doric portico at the front of Miro's recreated manor house. Though she stood shivering on the old Cotswold stone flag floor she didn't mind: rain meant the end of that oppressive heat. She could breathe again.

"I know it's summertime," she said. "But if we light the fire we can sit indoors together and listen to the storm."

Spurts of wind ruffled the surface of the lake. The darkening sky took all the colour from the water and Florian glanced irritably at the looming cloud while he dragged Miro's rowing boat to the water's edge. There would be no protection if it began to rain. Moving briskly he tied the boat, then heaved Alan's surprisingly heavy body up to drape it across the wooden side where the body folded at the stomach. He lifted the legs and swung the corpse down into the bottom of the boat, the legs resting on a seat. He went to the head of the boat and heaved on Alan's body till his legs flopped down from the seat and lay along the bottom, beside the length of concrete joist that Florian had brought with him. He tied Alan's legs to the joist—an awkward task since both the joist and Alan's legs were virtually unmovable in the cramped space. To be sure the legs would not come free, Florian used more rope than he needed, three separate lengths.

By the time he had finished he was sweating freely. He had a blister on one hand. As the first rain began to fall, Florian untied the guy rope and pushed off from the shallow shore. The boat sat low in the water and Florian felt he was rowing through treacle. Though the lake had no current it was hard to pull the boat away from the shore. But gradually, as the rain increased, he rowed the boat into the middle of the choppy lake.

Rain fell all about him, fizzing on the water. He was soaking wet. When he was far out into the middle he stopped, carefully shipped his oars, and began to edge Alan's ungainly mass up across the side. Pulling the body up was the easy part. Getting the legs over, tied as they were tied to a concrete joist, would be no joke. Florian paused. If he heaved the body over, and the concrete weight dragged it down to the lake floor, would it sink deep enough to be out of sight? How deep *was* the lake? He needed a plumb line, something to drop from the boat down to the bottom. He had some rope left but nothing to tie it to. He needed a weight. He looked around the boat. Apart from the wooden oars the only inanimate object—apart from Alan—was the concrete joist. But he couldn't use that. He could take a chance, of course—drop Alan over and assume the lake was deep. But was it?

Rain lashed the surface.

He freed one of his oars, and holding it tightly he leant over the other side from Alan and prodded down into the water towards the floor of the gravel pit. Nothing. But the oar was only about five feet long, six at most. Florian leant right out and prodded again, this time allowing his hands to dip beneath the surface, but although he encountered nothing he still couldn't be sure the lake bottom was not just below his oar. The only way to be sure was to dive in and swim down to try to reach it. He shook his head. What would it be like down there? There might be a forest of entangling weeds. He would be swimming in the dark. He wouldn't know what he was swimming amongst. He wouldn't know how far he had gone down.

A flash of lightning made him jump. How close was that? Thunder exploded. Florian ducked instinctively, his ears ringing. He had a vision of the boat illuminated on the lake. Would lightning pick him out as the highest point on the water? He dared not hang around. He heaved on Alan's dead weight and felt the concrete joist scrape the wooden hull. He paused again, rain lashing down. If he dropped Alan here and the water wasn't deep enough the corpse would float into a standing position, legs weighted to the lake bottom and head bobbing on the surface. He couldn't chance it. But wet as he was he was not going to dive down into that murky lake.

Lightning flashed again. He cowered. Thunder roared.

Florian scrabbled in the bottom of the rocking rowing boat, using his remaining piece of rope to tie Alan's wrists together and to then tie the wrists to the concrete joist until Alan was trussed like a pig on a roasting spit. He wouldn't float now. When the heavy joist sank to the bottom, Alan would remain clinging to it among the mud and weeds.

Another flash of lightning. The whole lake lit up. Before the light subsided Florian saw the entire surface alive with rain. A thunder clap.

Alan's bent body lay at the side of the rowing boat and the pale concrete joist lay along the wooden floor. Body and joist together were too heavy to lift. Florian heaved Alan along the floor of the boat, then manhandled one end of the joist onto the stout wooden cross seat. The boat rocked. Panting now, he hauled on the other end of the joist, lifting it up towards the rim of the boat. He paused for breath, anchored his feet against the far side, then heaved his end of the joist up clear of the gunwale, up again, up higher, pivoting the joist on the wooden seat. In the same movement he swung the joist round, bringing Alan's lumbering body up into the soaking air, so that both the body and joist crashed against the side of the boat, their weight carrying them over the side towards the churning water. The boat rocked sideways, and Florian pressed hard with his feet against the other side to steady it.

The foot of the joist slipped on the seat. The combined weight crunched at the rim. Florian could see the joist sliding back into the little rowing boat but he threw his own weight against the higher end and forced it out across the water. It seesawed drunkenly. He heard a sound of splintering wood and he threw himself out at the projecting end and forced it downwards towards the water. A crunching, splintering noise. A sudden movement. Water. The boat dipped over. The combined mass of Alan, Florian and the joist slid awkwardly into the water and sunk instantly. Florian was below the surface. He was being dragged down. He couldn't see. In the sudden slip he'd had no time to breathe. He clamped his mouth shut, screwed up his eyes. The lake sucked him down. He realised he was still holding the joist and he let go of it, kicking his legs, pulling with his arms in a frantic effort to reach the surface. A dash of coldness. A smack of air. He opened his eyes to find himself on the surface. He could see surprisingly well. He splashed, kicking his legs in case some unseen monster of the deep, some avenging ghoul, might clutch at his ankles and drag him down. Where was the boat? He couldn't see it. Had it toppled over?

Don't let the boat have sunk.

Then he saw it bobbing behind him. It was still upright. Sobbing with relief and gratitude, Florian swam the few yards to the little rowing boat and grabbed hold of the side. Now he had to get inside it—without scuttling it in the teeming water. He moved to the rear, draped his arms over the wooden rim and began to heave himself up. The boat dipped towards him. Florian kept central to the stern. As he pulled himself up out of the water, his weight was counterbalanced by the entire length of the boat. The boat heaved. The front rose from the lake. Florian kept his eye fixed on the prow as he climbed further from the water. Suddenly he had his chest, then his belly above the side, and he could pitch himself forwards. He banged his face, felt the boat rock again wildly. He panicked a moment as a foot of cold water splashed around his face. But it was only the water in the bottom of the boat.

Florian found the seat and sat staring around the lake. The rain was so strong now that he could hardly see beyond the boat—but inside the boat he could see both the oars still locked in place. He breathed with huge rasping sobs like an Olympic swimmer at the end of a hard race. His stomach hurt. He was alive.

Florian looked into the wall of rain. He waited but there was no flash of lightning. His skin streamed. There was so much rain now that to be out in the air was to be as wet as in the cold lake water. But he could breathe here. He wouldn't drown.

Finally came another flash of lightning—and when it did come it seemed almost an anticlimax. He paused, counted, till thunder came. Then he crawled along the boat and gathered the oars. That flash of light had been just enough to show a glimpse of shore.

The rain fell harder. Florian began rowing for the side of the lake. After several strokes his spirits rose. Rain didn't matter and the dark would hide him. As he rowed for home he began to sing. Alone on the water Florian bellowed his defiant song into the face of the raging storm.

Act Two

De Flores:

'Whatever ails me, now a-late especially,
I can as well be hanged as refrain from seeing her.
Some twenty times a day, nay, not so little,
Do I force errands, frame ways and excuses,
To come into her sight; and I've small reason for't,
And less encouragement, for she baits me still
Every time worse than other; does profess herself
The cruellest enemy to my face in town.
At no hand can abide the sight of me,
As if danger or ill-luck hung in my looks.'

The Changeling,
by Thomas Middleton & William Rowley

Act Two, Scene One.

Chapter 11

Miro took the call at dawn, waking groggily, sitting up, scrabbling for the phone and disturbing Joanna by his side. There was so little daylight it could have been dead of night. He could only grunt into the phone: "Yes, yes. I'll—when?"

He thumped it down. Jo propped herself on her elbow to mumble a question but Miro was easing himself from bed, cursing someone—the world in general, the weather. "You awake?" he asked unnecessarily.

"I am now."

He stomped across the room and tugged the curtains apart. It was raining. Sodden clouds hung black and low. "Look at it."

"What's the matter?" Jo asked.

"Bloody rain."

He stood naked, a dim shape at the window. "All I need."

She waited, but he said no more. She saw him look at her, his expression unreadable in the dimness, although it seemed to her he looked embarrassed. He left the window and began stumbling around the room to find his clothes. She turned the bedside light on. He grunted, "Thanks."

"What is it?" she asked again.

"Oh." He shook his head.

She swung her legs down to the floor. "If you're getting dressed I'll make some coffee."

He had found a business suit and as he climbed into the trousers he said, "Ring Florian. Get him up."

"Florian?" she repeated faintly.

He zipped his pants. "*I'll* do it. Have to do everything myself."

She was in the kitchen warming her hands on the freshly made cafetiere when Florian walked in. He nodded and she stared back at him. "Well?"

If Florian had dressed hastily he showed no sign of it. He wore a sombre sports jacket, white shirt and tie, and his shoes shone like an officer's in the Marines. But that face—an injured officer. She tightened her dressing gown. "What happened last night?"

He glanced beyond her, then walked quickly to the inner door and peeped through. "Good morning, Miro."

He turned back to her and shrugged meaningfully. "Is the coffee ready?" he asked loudly.

She could hear Miro in the hall. "It needs a minute yet."

As Miro barged in, Florian moved deferentially to the wall. "Shocking weather today, sir, isn't it?"

"Don't even mention the bloody weather. Are we ready? Right, let's go."

"Have some coffee," Jo said.

"No time."

"I've just made it."

Miro glanced at her apologetically. "I've got to get on—you know?"

"It's filthy out," said Florian.

"Don't tell me."

Florian said, "We might be grateful for a warm cup of coffee." He smiled at Jo. "Especially since it's made."

Miro sighed. "Is the car ready?"

"Of course."

Jo said, "Whatever it is can wait while you snatch breakfast."

"I don't want any."

"That coffee does smell good," said Florian.

Jo quickly spread cups and saucers and pushed the plunger of the cafetiere. "Hope it's done," she said.

Florian stepped forward. "Would anyone like milk?"

Seated at the kitchen table, Miro seemed less stressed. The coffee was too hot to drink immediately and although he had said he wouldn't eat, Jo quickly made some toast. She busied herself buttering it while the two men sat opposite each other on kitchen chairs.

Florian said, "Two of the finest aromas in the world—toast and fresh coffee. Almost worth getting up early for."

Miro said, "Far too early to eat."

"We should take every opportunity presented to us," said Florian, adding, "as my mother used to say."

"You had a mother, did you?"

Florian chuckled—not because Miro was amusing but to encourage him to talk. "If it's to be a busy morning we'll be glad we had this toast."

"I don't want it." Miro sipped the coffee, still too hot. "And we can get coffee when we're there."

"Not as fine as Joanna makes."

Florian looked so relaxed at the kitchen table they could have all been sharing Sunday breakfast. "At this time of day there'll be no traffic, and once we're on our way we'll make good time." He was aware of Jo staring pointedly from behind Miro's back but he didn't react. "Two minutes more won't hurt."

Miro couldn't sit still. He straightened his already well-knotted tie, then began patting his pockets as if ticking off a mental inventory. Florian smiled across the table. "Got everything?" he asked. "Spectacles, testicles, watch and wallet?"

Miro nodded and tried the coffee again.

Jo went to Miro and placed both hands upon his shoulders. "What's so important that lets them drag you out at crack of dawn?"

He shook his head as if a fly buzzed round his ear. She began gently massaging his shoulders, staring at Florian over his head, and said, "You mustn't keep secrets from me. I've a right to know."

Miro grunted. He swallowed some coffee, then said, "This bloody weather brought it to light."

Florian glanced at her, then put down his cup to listen as Miro continued. "Bloody rain. God. You know the supermarket—that problem with the Goods Inwards door?"

Jo murmured. Florian relaxed and leant forward in his chair, lacing his fingers beneath his chin to listen complacently. Not his problem.

"We had to dig out the tarmac, remember? Make a dip so their damn oversize lorries could squeeze through. Well, what d'you think happens when it rains?"

Jo was still kneading his shoulders. "Isn't there a soakaway?"

Miro snorted. "Well, you'd think so. I mean, you're not an architect, yet even *you'd* put in a soakaway. It's obvious. Dig a dip, it fills with water. Obvious. Christ! And I pay these people. I can't *believe* their stupidity."

"It did rain last night," mused Florian.

"It's still raining. Goods Inwards is flooded. Can you imagine? I don't want to think about it."

Jo pulled a wry face. "You're doing nothing else."

"So the entrance doorway flooded," said Florian, interested now, "then overflowed through the stockroom? How deep is it?"

"God knows." Miro stood up. "Let's get down there."

Miro gulped the last of his coffee. Florian stood up to join him and murmured, "Dry goods and rain water. My, my."

Jo giggled. "They'll need a salvage sale. In their first week."

"Cost a fortune," Miro snapped.

Florian said, "Mind you, if they stored the soap powder at floor level they'll have a very clean stockroom by now."

"Fish will start leaping from the freezer," said Jo.

"It's not funny!" Miro shouted.

"No." She tried to look serious. Behind Miro's back Florian mimed a swimming motion. Jo looked away, then hastily began clearing cups from the table. Miro stomped from the room.

"In at the deep end," said Florian.

The day remained squally. By the time Jo had dressed, the rain had stopped and a brief period of sun was raising steam from the puddles. But by the time she returned downstairs it had started raining again. She opened the back door and watched the effect of wind across wet cobbles. She welcomed rain. Suddenly she shrugged and stepped out into the courtyard to let the fresh mist of rainwater play against her cheeks. She wandered up and down in it, opening herself to wetness. She danced a little jig and sang the chorus of *Singing in the Rain*. What the hell? No one was watching. She was alone at the house. She could dance naked and no one would care.

She skipped along the wet cobbles to stand in front of the glass-fronted annex. She tried the door but it was locked. Because Florian had his room there, the entire building was out of bounds. No one came for business meetings and the conservatory, with its formal reception area plants, was a place that only Florian used. The rooms behind the conservatory remained unoccupied. The whole annex was a folly.

Jo stood on the cobbles and pressed her body against the glass wall. She could see indoor plants standing stiffly in the darkness, a couple of cane chairs no one ever sat in, a piece of garden statuary of a cherub balanced on one toe. Emptiness. Unused.

Her clothes were wet but she didn't mind: she could change them—what else had she to do? While the rain continued she wandered around the side of the house to the front. The lawns were green again. Rose bushes hung heavy with water. The sky was awash with colour, an English sky, a watercolourist's sky. A living sky. Jo looked along the drive towards Miro's flamboyant gates. No traffic passed. No one was out there. Yet for some reason she had a sudden, disturbing memory of Alan, startling her at the front steps of the house, saying, "On your own, I'm glad to see."

What had happened last night? In the kitchen this morning Florian's face gave nothing away. Had he met with Alan? Would he keep him away from her? She glanced again at the iron gate. If Florian had bungled it last night or if, as was more likely, Alan chose to ignore Florian's warning, he might come back again today. Knowing Alan, that was just what he would do.

Suddenly the garden seemed less welcoming. Jo felt wet clothes sticking to her skin. When she returned to the house she locked the back door and stayed inside.

Towards lunchtime she was bored. The morning had dragged on. Miro, engrossed in his flooded supermarket, had not bothered to ring, and the squally weather couldn't decide between sun and heavy showers. She wandered around the silent house, trying every room, looking down into the gardens from each window. It was strange to think she would soon be living here, and she could see Miro's concern that she would tire of it—tire of *him* was his worry, but she was happy with Miro; it was the empty house that would get her down. People were not meant to live in it on their own. This was a house that should ring with servants and children, a family house. There should be the clatter of horses' hooves on cobbles, people moving from room to room, someone's radio, an occasional voice. But there were no voices, no phone calls.

The rain had stopped again. As clouds scudded away the sun swelled and blazed again, a golden Aphrodite from the sea. The sky shone like wet forget-me-nots. Jo opened the front door and went out to feel the full impact of that sun. The lawns were greener now, marshlike, and on every branch of the drooping roses hung sparkling droplets of heavy rain. Petals had been beaten from the roses, and they lay in battered pulp on the formal beds. As she walked between puddles on the drive the air smelt fresh and clean.

She heard the front gates opening.

Jo waited by the shimmering rose bushes and watched the Lexus glide up the drive. Florian sat in the car alone, which meant that Miro must have dealt with the supermarket and gone on to his office. He wouldn't need Florian till late afternoon.

Jo was nervous. She had been alone with Florian before but always when he was a servant who could be ignored. Now she was waiting for him. She had been waiting for him all morning. For his news.

She watched the car continue round the back.

She could follow him to the garages or she could wait at

111

the front till he appeared. Assuming he did appear. No, he had to come to her—he was *her* servant now. He had always been a servant, Miro's servant—the only thing that had changed was that now he was her servant too. She would wait for him. He had seen her. He would come to her. He had his duties to report.

Florian and Jo walked together in the rain-bedecked sunken garden at the west side of the house. The midday sun shone between blobs of fast-moving cloud and where they walked the dipping fronds of Victorian ferns hung wet and scented on old stone flags. Between the broken stones sprawled loose clouds of alchemilla mollis and in the central raised bed were heavy peonies past their prime.

Florian nodded at the saturated plants. "One of my many tasks—keeping this unruly mob at bay. I haven't the time, of course, so I practise Darwinian gardening, letting only the strongest survive. I get rid of unwanted weeds."

He looked at her slyly. He was making small talk to see how long her patience lasted. He wouldn't say what she wanted to hear; he would make her ask.

"Did you see him?"

"I did."

"And?"

"I carried out my task."

She ran her fingers against a low moss-covered wall.

"What did he say?"

"Very little."

Florian tugged at some fumitory growing in the wall. "Surprising how strong this is. I keep rooting it out but I can't get rid of it."

"Will he bother me again?"

Florian stared at her. "No, you can rest assured that Mr.

Pirie will never bother you again."

She gasped in relief. Suddenly she turned away, raised a hand to her moist eye and moved into the deep shade of a monkey puzzle tree at the end of the sunken garden. Normally it was dry beneath this tree but after the night of heavy rain the ground was dank.

"Can I be sure of that?" she asked, not looking at him.

"As sure as that this tree will outlive both of us."

She shivered and moved back into the sun.

"Joanna?"

"I'm sorry," she said, wiping her eye. "It's silly, but when you hear news you've waited for, it sometimes makes you cry."

Florian moved swiftly to touch her arm, but she pulled away. They were both in sunlight now. "I have a token for you," he said.

"For me?"

"Proof." His head angled mischievously. "It was sent somewhat unwillingly." He pulled something from his pocket. "But I couldn't get the ring without the finger."

With a flourish he unwrapped his handkerchief and held it out to her. For a moment she stared without realising what she saw—then she stepped back sharply. "What have you done?"

A trace of blood had glued the grey and puckered finger to Florian's handkerchief and it lay awkwardly, its severed knuckle stuck to the fabric and the bitten fingernail strangely pale. The ring had lost its shine, and shone dully. When Florian touched the cotton material the finger quivered as if admonishing her. She put a hand to her mouth.

Florian seemed genuinely surprised. "Is cutting off his finger worse than killing the whole man? He could have lived without his finger."

She made herself speak. "I gave him that ring."

"I made him send it back again."

"You really killed him?" Jo breathed.

He seemed unconcerned by her alarm. "I didn't want to leave the ring, and dead men have no use for jewellery, but he wouldn't part with it! Look, it's still stuck—as if the flesh and ring were one."

Florian smiled brightly as the sun went in again.

She said, "For God's sake, bury the finger. I'll take the ring."

He grinned. "I had thought of selling it. What's it worth?"

"Nothing. A trinket. I'll buy it from you—what do you want?"

"I've told you what I want."

"How much?" she faltered.

"Money—you think I did this for wages?" He laughed and turned away from her. "I committed murder for you, Jo, and your boyfriend gave his *life* for you. Can there be anything so precious you wouldn't give in return?"

"I don't understand."

He shook his head, walked several paces, then turned to face her once again. "What do you think I want?"

She tried not to understand. "Will . . . will five thousand pounds be enough? I don't know what these things cost—"

His face changed. "I could have hired a thug for less!" he shouted.

"You want more? I—"

"I could have slept at home in peace."

"I'll double the money—"

"You'll double my anger."

A sudden breeze shook the branches of the tree. Spots of rainwater fell on her dress, and when she moved away he followed her down the slippery stone path. They were back in the fern garden now. Wet green fronds slapped against their shins.

"Forget the money," Florian said. "You can't buy me off. You're in this as deep as I am."

"Not true," said Jo, hurrying away.

He grabbed her elbow. "Don't you want his ring?"

"I said bury it."

"It's engraved with both your names."

She tried to pull away but Florian would not let her. "And I have your note to him."

She hesitated—then turned, her eyes ablaze. "No, I told you to give the note to Alan."

"You think I'm mad? I have your note, in your handwriting, asking him to meet you secretly last night. I have his address you carefully wrote for me, in your own handwriting."

"In your book! *Your* book. You're in this too."

"Isn't that exactly what I said? We're in this jointly. You and I." His face was close to hers. He seemed to be declaiming these mad lines, she thought. His accent was more pronounced: "We must seal our relationship with a kiss."

She struggled away but he kept his grip on her. "How dare you?" she whispered.

"I dared more than this last night."

"This is . . . outrageous. How can you ask such a thing?"

He took her chin in his free hand. "What did *you* ask of me?"

"Not to murder."

"To stop him, to *guarantee* he couldn't harm you. Well, I've fulfilled my part, haven't I? But you seem reluctant to pay my fee—"

"*Seem* reluctant!"

He gently twisted her face, gazing intently into her eyes.

115

"You're not a virgin, Jo. Who will know?"

"I'm getting *married*—"

"You won't be the first wife to betray her husband."

"I can't."

"You can't refuse."

He turned his head to hide his inflamed scar from her, then he dipped and kissed her savagely on the mouth. She tried to move her head but Florian held it clamped in his strong hand. He forced his tongue between her lips. When he had finished she wiped her mouth three times. Angry tears sparkled in her eyes. Suddenly her lips moved to spit at him, but Florian clapped his hand across her mouth.

"Well, Jo—are you going to report me to Miro?" He paused, then released his hand. "Or shall *I* tell him?"

"Please, Florian, don't do this."

"Soft words for me at last."

He reached into his pocket, pulled out the crumpled handkerchief and placed it and the finger in her hand. He chuckled. "With this ring I do thee wed."

She recoiled and her first reaction was to throw the rag away. But he clenched her hand and moved the dirty bundle to the pocket of her skirt. Florian pushed the dead finger inside as deep as it would go, stroking her leg as he did so and lingering on her thigh. Jo was fighting back her tears.

He said, "You must sleep with me tonight, Jo. No more evasions."

"But I'll be with Miro—"

"Tell him that for these last nights before your marriage you want to sleep alone."

"I can't."

"You can sleep with me now, if you prefer."

"I'd rather sleep with a snake."

He laughed and pulled her close to him. He kissed her

once more briefly, then deliberately, watching her all the while, he placed his dark hand on her breast. He squeezed it softly through her shirt, and left his hand there. "Ssh. Hide your blushes in my chest. I feel you panting—and I tell you: before long you'll be panting for me in earnest."

Rain beat against the bedroom window as the sun suddenly emerged again, its bright golden light sparkling through beads of water running down the glass. A square of light fell across the bed and the room which had seemed chill began to warm again, the tangled daytime sheets turned cream, and her pine furniture glinted in the sun. Glancing from the bed they saw the sky dark in the upper window, pale blue below. The blue section grew larger and the edge of the cloud was etched with yellow.

"There'll be a rainbow," she said but they didn't move.

They lay entwined, his arm beneath her, his face nuzzling her hair. She was on her back, gazing at the window as the wind pushed the high cloud away. She was utterly relaxed and as the sun warmed the room she began to imagine herself on a Caribbean beach, her muscles aching from a swim while a restoring sun bathed her tired and relaxed body. The sound of his breath close to her ear could have been the sea. She moved her hand across his rump.

He grunted slightly and for a moment showed no other reaction. But he was satiated—twice last night, and again this lunchtime. His urgent need had gone but he lifted his leg and thumped his tired thigh across her own. He shifted onto her, and she whispered, "Come on, big boy, one more time."

He stopped the moment he was spent, wilting so fast she felt him slither away like something expelled. But it didn't matter: they were satisfied again. He grunted, rolled off and flopped onto his back.

"I can't keep *this* up," Jasper chuckled.

"You're doing great."

They lay comfortably exhausted in a tangle of knotted sheets and watched the light change in her bedroom as the clouds flitted across the sun. He had come back with her last night, stayed till two, and they had agreed they would drive back to her flat at lunchtime for one more turn. But they'd had two turns now—and still no lunch, he realised.

He asked if she had to return to work.

"Too late now. How about you?"

"I did everything I had to do this morning."

"What *do* you do?"

"Oh, you know. We could stay here all afternoon."

"Hm. You're married, aren't you?"

"Do you mind?"

"Will *she* mind?"

"She'll never know." He peeped round at her. "Will she?"

"Not from me. She and I wouldn't have much to talk about, anyway. Though, on the other hand . . ."

He peeped again to make sure that she was joking.

Dee said, "Don't worry. I won't spoil your life. A little sex outside marriage won't hurt anyone."

Chapter 12

Miro said, "OK, there are only three days till the wedding. Perhaps it's better we spend these final nights apart. It'll help mark out a difference."

She hadn't expected him to give in so easily. "I'm being silly."

His hand lay on her arm. "It's only till Saturday—doing this will make the wedding day more special."

"I don't want you to think—"

"We'll come to each other as strangers. Almost!" He chuckled. "That's how it ought to be."

He was firm. He wouldn't be shifted. But what she hadn't expected was that, after supper, he would tell Florian to drive her home.

"No, Miro please—can't *you* drive me?"

"It's what I employ him for." Miro had looked her deep in the eyes. "I know you don't like Florian, but he's a good man. Do try to get used to him. I'd hate to have to let him go."

"And would you?"

"Certainly, if you absolutely can't get on with him. You *don't* like him, do you?"

"No," she whispered.

But there was no way she could refuse to let his chauffeur drive her home. There was no way she could avoid sitting in the car with Florian as he drove her through the dusk.

"This is nice," he said, once they'd gone out through the gate.

"It wasn't my idea."

He chuckled. "Surely you don't want to sleep all by yourself?"

She closed her eyes. "Look, you got what you wanted this afternoon, and that's an end to it."

He flicked the wipers to intermittent. Theirs was the only car on the road.

He said, "We *started* this afternoon."

"No way! You named your price. You got it."

He was driving quickly along the deserted country road. "I wonder if Miro will wait up for me."

"Of course!" she said quickly. "He'll notice if you get back late."

"Why? Did you say something that might make him suspicious?"

She didn't answer.

"No Joanna, he won't think anything. As long as I'm there with the car in the morning, he will be fine."

"You can't stay all night!"

"How long *can* I stay?"

It was almost a minute before she spoke. "What happened this afternoon was a one-off. You forced me, but never again."

"Didn't you like it?"

"I hate you. I don't know why I . . . We have to be sensible. I'm getting *married* in three days. You know this can't go on."

"You're right, my *love*—we do have to be sensible. Though with Miro out at work all day, we shouldn't find that too hard."

"I'm not going near you again!"

Florian slammed his foot on the brake. "Get out."

"What?" She huddled in the back.

He turned. "Easiest way to settle this. Get out of the car."

They were in a lonely dark Wiltshire lane. Soft rain misted against the outside of the car. When Florian switched off the engine there was not a single light to be seen. The clouded windows made the darkness denser.

She said, "You can't abandon me here. What d'you think Miro would say?"

"Who said anything about abandoning you?"

"Switch the car on. *Florian.*"

He said, "Get out and lean against the car. I'll fuck you there."

"You won't!"

Thick darkness hugged the car.

He said, "It'll be good in the fresh air."

"No."

He sighed. "OK, I'll *drag* you out. You like it rough?"

"This is ridiculous."

"You'd better get this into your head, Joanna: I shall fuck you tonight. And tomorrow night I'll fuck you again. I may not get you on your wedding night but I'll fuck you afterwards. You're mine now. You'll be Miro's wife but we'll share you."

She shook her head in silence. She could hear soft rain on the car roof.

He said, "If we pop out now and do it against the car we can do it nice and quick. You'll get a good night's sleep, I'll get home early, and Miro won't have to wonder what's going on."

"You can't . . ."

"I know it's wet, Jo—damp, really, you can't call this wet. Last night though, that was wet. Believe me, I was soaked. But I'm not doing it *inside* the car. It's too cramped and I do

121

like a bit of space. Anyway, we might leave a stain on Miro's seat—" She let out a sob. "So really, it would be better back at your place—more comfortable." Florian laughed. "Oh come on, Jo, don't make such a drama—it's only sex. You like it really."

"I hate it. I hate *you*."

"Really? There was a moment this afternoon, wasn't there—when you started to let go?"

She began to cry. His voice softened. "Don't do that, Joanna. I don't like to see you cry."

Her lips seemed paralysed. She could hardly speak. "Look . . . I let you this afternoon but I won't do it again."

"You will."

"You'll have to rape me."

"Mhm, you do like it rough. I thought so."

"Alan raped me. But yours is a worse rape. He was at least my boyfriend."

"I'm more than just a boyfriend, Jo—you owe me. But don't worry, I won't rape you. I won't use violence."

"There's no other way you'll have me again."

"Oh yes there is. You'll come to me willingly."

"I won't."

"Maybe not this time. But you will soon."

The silence in the flat was deafening. When she realised it was the silence that oppressed her she went straight to the stereo and switched it on. But it didn't work—the music irritated her. She changed to something classical but that didn't work either. Any kind of noise got on her nerves. Just as the silence got on her nerves. What she wanted was to hear a voice—his voice. Did that mean she was falling in love with him? No, good God—she shook her head and turned off the stereo. She had spent last night with Jasper, most of today, and now that he had finally gone, the sudden silence was as if the electric power had failed. Well, Dee thought, I certainly won't need a candle! It was just that, as in any new affair, they had talked and talked. They had talked in the restaurant—how long ago that seemed—they had talked in bed until the small hours, they had talked all afternoon and evening, they had continued talking even as she leant into his car to kiss goodbye. Then suddenly he'd gone. The sound had been switched off. Now the flat seemed to resonate to invisible audio waves she couldn't hear.

She felt lifeless. Dee was used to talk. She spent her day chatting to invisible clients on the telephone, to colleagues and friends, to anyone. Sometimes she thought that she used her vocal chords more than anyone she knew. If when they were born, people were issued with a finite store of words she would have emptied all hers now. She felt empty. She felt sore, physically sore from almost twenty-four hours of bruising sex. She looked at the flat and saw two empty wine bottles, several glasses, five plates, some open food cartons. The bed was a wreck. The kitchen looked as if it had been ransacked.

It was eleven o'clock. Not late, not really late, not too late to begin clearing away the mess—but too damn late for Dee. She would get up early tomorrow morning and sort it then. Or she could leave it till tomorrow night—but no: Jasper would be coming round. God knows what excuses he'd tell at home. One thing Dee never had to worry about, all those lies. He was married, she was not. Their affair would have to be kept secret but it wasn't her concern. He seemed nice enough and as long as they could be open with each other she didn't care what secrets they kept from anyone else.

She looked at the mess again and realised she wasn't tired enough for bed. She seemed to have been in bed for hours.

For days, it felt. She began desultorily collecting dirty crockery and carrying it through to the kitchenette. It wouldn't be a long affair, she knew. He was married, and he would soon run out of excuses to tell his wife. And though they'd been to the restaurant last night and down to the pub this evening, he'd soon decide he couldn't take the risk of being seen out with her. The affair would close in on itself. It would last as long as the sex was great, or until one of them started blaming the other for imagined grievances. Until one of them could no longer stand the sight of the pair of them festering in her little flat. Every love nest gets soiled eventually.

But in this early stage the sex *was* great. Afternoon in bed, evening on the floor. Far too much booze. Dee brought all the clutter into the kitchenette and as she stooped to place pieces in the dishwasher she felt a draught beneath her skirt. For a moment she thought nothing of it, and then realised she wasn't wearing panties. She shrugged wryly, wondering where she'd left them. Then she remembered their naughty capers coming back from the pub. Naughty Jasper, invigorated by fresh air. When he pulled down her panties he had put them for safe keeping in his pocket. Where they almost certainly still were.

How would he explain them to his wife?

Jo lay in bed, staring at the ceiling. Though she had the lights out, enough of a streetlamp glow came through the curtains to dimly illuminate the room. There was a crack in the curtains and a sharp line of burnt yellow ran across the ceiling and bent down the facing wall. It was irritating but Jo hadn't the energy to get up and fix it. No energy at all. Her body ached and her lips felt as if she had been punched on the mouth. Between her legs felt violated, as if Florian had pushed his hands in and pulled her apart. She had a tremor in her thigh. The room was silent now that he'd left her, and she lay on the crumpled bed like a discarded rag doll. She could smell sex on her sheets. She could smell Florian. She'd have to change all the bed linen, throw it in the washing machine and fetch some new. In a minute. Not now. What was she going to do? She couldn't tell Miro, she couldn't tell anyone, she couldn't see any way out. If only this hadn't happened. She kept going back through the chain of events that had brought her here but it seemed that she had never had a choice. Tonight, this afternoon, yesterday, the day Alan had called. The affair with Alan two years ago. The baby. If she hadn't met Alan she would not have got pregnant, there would have been no abortion and nothing with which Alan could have threatened her on his return. Even so, she should have faced him out. She should have told Miro and by doing so, drawn Alan's sting. Instead, she had told Florian—how *could* she have been so stupid? She'd been desperate, of course. But she hadn't realised what Florian would do. Had she?

She had known that he meant violence but had refused to take it in. Just as she had refused to hear his price. He hadn't really been ambiguous. What had he asked for? Something precious. "A dangerous service deserves a precious reward." Was that ambiguous?

He had been on her mind all last night. In the garden with Miro she knew that at that very moment Florian was confronting Alan. In bed with Miro she wondered what happened between them. She couldn't sleep for worrying. There had been a storm, and the lashing rain had echoed the churning images in her brain. And this morning the first thing she had asked Florian in the kitchen was whether he had done it. *It*—what did she think that he had done? What did she hope he'd done?

She should never have sent him. That was the time to have stopped it—not this morning. By the time Florian appeared in the garden to claim his reward she was immersed too far. After last night she had no choice: Florian had done as she had asked and it was time for her to pay the price. She had never allowed herself to look ahead—just as this afternoon she had let herself believe that by going to bed with Florian *once* she would settle the debt. It had seemed reasonable. He had named his price, asked for something precious, and she'd given the most precious thing she possessed. That's what he'd said. But what he *hadn't* said, and more tellingly what Joanna had not asked, was what would happen next. He was blackmailing her; it was simple as that. Like every blackmailer, he would never stop. She groaned. Whenever she read of blackmailers or saw them in films she sneered at the gullibility of their victims, seriously imagining that by paying a price they could buy the blackmailer off. Now she was entangled in the selfsame snare.

There was no way out.

Three days to the wedding—would he come to her every night? Yes, he had already insisted she must sleep with him again. It was the price she had to pay. She hated Florian—that he could do this to her, that she had let him. That she had gone to his private room in the annex, taken off her clothes, lain on his bed and allowed him to take possession of her. She had tried to lie inert but he had goaded her, prodding and shaking her into resistance, saying he wanted to see her become spirited and alive. The way he'd pleasured himself in every cranny of her body. He had done things to her that no man had done before. It was as if her lack of resistance encouraged him to try anything he'd ever dreamed of—lying her face up, face down, on top, below, licking every part of her, making Jo lick him. Experimenting with her like a brand new toy.

126

And tonight, when he had invaded her in her own bed, he came not as an experimenter but as if he and she were long established lovers. He had undressed her, caressed her, asked her to caress him—showing her ways she had never tried before, that she never knew existed. But of course, she thought, he hadn't been doing those things to arouse *her*, he had done them to re-arouse himself. He'd had her twice this afternoon and he needed extra stimulation to perform again tonight. And yet he'd behaved as if he wanted to excite her. Perhaps he had. Perhaps he thought he could make her want him. But he repelled her. Jo shuddered and turned over on her side. She would never want him. He might make her *do* it again—

She gasped. She realised that she would have to do it again with Florian any time he asked. For as long into the future as he decided. She moved on the bed, wrapping herself into a tight foetal position, slipping her thumb into her mouth. Again. He'd want her again. And again. And he'd want her to want him—that had been his intention tonight as he had stroked her, whispered to her, put his tongue in her ear, worked down her body, sucked on her nipples—no: tongued them, that was the word—kissed her navel, then worked, oh so slowly down. She knew he had wanted a reaction but she wouldn't give him one. He was a bastard. He had even made her kiss his livid scar.

But she hadn't yielded. She had lain as stiffly as possible, hands by her side, eyes averted. Given him no satisfaction. Given him *nothing*. Except that her body let her down. The things that Florian had done to her—his hands and probing fingers—she couldn't help if she had sometimes responded. Twice she had caught herself thrusting back. She'd had to rip her hands from his back. But when he reached his climax—*shouting* at her, for Heaven's sake—she hadn't reached hers, and she had shown him. She had lain inert, barely panting.

No reaction. No satisfaction. Arrogance in her eyes.

She was tight in a ball now, burrowing her head in the knotted pillow, breathing the residual stink of him, sucking hard on her thumb. She was dampening below. *Now,* as if he'd finally turned her on! No. No.

He mustn't come to her again. He mustn't do this.

Chapter 13

Her wedding dress was encased in polythene. To prevent it creasing, Jo had hung it outside the wardrobe door, her satin shoes beneath. She looked at it hanging stiffly and imagined herself wearing it—it wasn't hard to do: she'd had so many fittings, had stared at herself in the shop mirror so many times, it had become a familiar picture. All that fiddling—a tuck here, a tiny adjustment there—to create a dress she would wear just once. All that fuss.

She should encase her *flat* in polythene. Miro had still not agreed that she could keep it. He couldn't see the point of her maintaining a drab little flat she would never live in. He had even asked if she were having doubts—was she not committed to their marriage? She'd had to reassure him, which was slightly tiresome, but Miro hadn't understood why she needed this little bolt-hole. "You'll be living with me."

But that was *his* house. Everyone had their own place: Miro had Electra Court, Dee had her flat—even Florian had his room in the annex. But she would have nowhere. She would always be a guest. She would be like that wedding dress—out on display but empty inside. She touched it, but it felt unreal in its polythene. She could take it out, put it on again, but . . . wasn't it unlucky to wear the dress before the day? She had tried it in the shop—many times—but to wear the dress in her flat, to walk around the rooms alone in it, did

129

not seem right. She sighed. Being on her own did not seem right. The truth was that she was no longer comfortable anywhere on her own: when she was in Miro's house either he was there, in which case she wasn't on her own, or she *was* alone and the house was empty, in which case she felt ill at ease; or worse, Florian was there, in which case . . . She shivered. She couldn't even be comfortable in her flat, because it had ceased to be her private bolt-hole. Florian had right of entry. He had even asked for a key! It was the only thing she had refused him.

He had claimed his right again today. She had known he would. This might be the day before her wedding but it hadn't stopped him. He had brought her back from the bridal boutique, had carried the dress box up the communal stairs, had followed her through the front door as polite as any footman—and had then pushed her on the bed and had his way with her.

But he'd said he would stay away tonight. Jo didn't know whether it was out of a warped consideration for the fact that she was marrying the next day or whether Miro had commanded his service for final chores. But tonight, for the first time since he had ravished her in this very bedroom, she could go to bed peacefully in her own good time. She would sleep alone. Neither Miro nor Florian would trouble her tonight. Peaceful indeed, yet odd—because in a curious way Jo felt unsettled. She touched the dress again, then went around the flat to turn off unwanted lights. The bedside lamp gave a cosy glow. It looked almost romantic—at one time she had thought it *was* romantic. Back when she believed in romance.

In the shaded light her bridal dress changed colour. Peachy white. Crisp, unlived-in. Tomorrow she would parade in that dress in Miro's village church. The dress would come out of its polythene and she would become Mrs. Miro

Vermont. Jo sat on her bed and began to undress.

When she was fully undressed she reached automatically for her chaste white night-dress, but hesitated. Why did she wear such a prissy thing? What was the point of this flimsy rubbish? It didn't keep out the cold but, coming from Marks and Spencers, neither did it look remotely sexy—it was just a skein between her breasts and the duvet. It preserved her modesty. Ha! As if she had any modesty to preserve. Anyway, she thought, there was no one to see her, so it didn't matter whether she looked modest or sexy. The nightie was an irritating gauze that would tangle round her as she tried to sleep.

She slipped into bed naked.

She shivered happily beneath the pleasantly cool cotton duvet. Why didn't she always go to bed nude? She would in the future. Jo stretched luxuriously. She looked around the room, then switched off the lamp. A change of lighting. It felt so peaceful to lie alone in bed. She glanced around the darkened room, then closed her eyes and snuggled into the pillow. Such peace. Here in the pillow she could smell Florian's scent, a mix of aftershave and sweat. Was it aftershave? He never seemed to shave. Perhaps he didn't. Or perhaps he only shaved half his face.

She could definitely smell his fragrance. It was unavoidable: he had been here every day and she couldn't be bothered to wash out the bedclothes every day. She had washed them the first time, but he'd come back. He seemed to prefer to use her flat. Perhaps he thought the annex too dangerous. Perhaps he liked to invade her territory, to get inside her bolt-hole. She smiled briefly. Well, you had to laugh.

Was there any chance he'd come tonight? He never announced his visits. No, he wouldn't: not even Florian would sully her wedding eve. She listened. Nothing. She imagined him creeping up the stairs now, knocking at her door. What if she pretended she hadn't heard him? He wouldn't go away—he'd just knock louder. She'd have to get up in case the neighbours heard. Though she was naked, of course. How would he react if she opened the door stark naked? He'd think he'd won, of course.

She listened to the silence. Little traffic tonight. Strange, for Friday night—and it was wet outside: that usually encouraged traffic. People didn't want to walk out in the rain. Two cars went by, then a police siren somewhere far away, followed by silence again. Relative silence. Like the uncanny silence over Alan's disappearance. No one had said anything, no one appeared to notice. He had just vanished from sight, leaving nothing but the ring. His finger—that sick-minded Florian, cutting off his finger.

Jo sat up in bed sharply. *She still had Alan's finger!*

She was in the kitchenette with the light out. At first she'd left it on but she couldn't shake the vision of herself illuminated at the kitchen window, a bright rectangle of light blazing out into the darkness, herself sharply delineated in her woolly dressing gown while she placed Alan's withered finger on a chopping board and used a carving knife to hack off the ring. So she switched off the light and worked in the dark. As she used the knife she found that his flesh melted away quite easily now, soft and putrid, but pieces of gristle clung around the knuckles. For endless terrifying seconds it looked as if she would still not be able to slide the ring from Alan's finger, that she might have to throw the whole thing in a saucepan and boil the flesh away. She was panicking, of course. With the kitchen counter bathed in dim half light from the street she began to work more patiently, until she could prise the reluctant ring away. She threw it in the sink, ran hot water, left it running while she considered what to do with the scraps and bones. Such tiny, delicate bones. Alan used to have large, well-muscled hands, a fighter's hands, yet these slivers of finely chiselled bone seemed so fragile that one punch would have snapped any one of them in two.

What to do with them? She turned to the ring, washed it thoroughly in the scalding water and tossed it on the draining board to dry. She picked up one of Alan's finger bones, the larger, and used it to scrape flakes of flesh into the sink. Running water took them to the plug-hole but two of the pieces were too large to go straight down. She poked at them with the bone. One flushed away, but the other sat bobbing in the outlet. She'd have to cut it smaller.

Jo took the carving knife and speared the stubborn, rubbery flesh. She placed it back on the chopping board and diced it into several pieces, wondering whether it had been wise to flush the flesh down the drain. If by any ghastly chance the pieces stuck somewhere they'd remain as evidence. But would anyone recognise them for what they had been? No. Well, too late now, she couldn't go back. She flushed all the last scraps away. If only the sink had been fitted with a waste disposal unit. If only a lot of things. She left hot water running while she washed the board. It seemed clean but she couldn't tell. Germs and microbes were too small to see. But they'd still be there. She squirted soap liquid on the board but even as she began scrubbing she knew she'd never reuse that board. She couldn't chop fresh meat on a board that she'd used to dissect Alan's finger. She'd have to throw it away.

Where? It was evidence too. The board would fit in the kitchen trash bin but inside that plastic liner its shape would be large and obvious. Where else could she put it? If she threw it in the bins outside it would lie unwrapped and exposed to view. It would be less conspicuous in the bin if she wrapped it in a newspaper. A chopping board was hardly evidence. She felt more comfortable now in the dim half light as she checked there were no remaining traces of Alan's finger. Everything gone. Just like him. No one had remarked on his disappearance. Perhaps no one would. No—that wasn't being realistic, and she had to be realistic. Alan would be missed eventually and his disappearance would be investigated. The investigation might lead to her. There must be no trace of him in her flat. She began washing her hands. Alan's flesh was gone, the board was scrubbed and would be thrown away, the bones . . . She ought to hide them more efficiently. She shouldn't put them in the kitchen trash. Where to put them? Somewhere outside. Was there anything else she should do first?

She took a duster, went into the living room and began rubbing at the wooden surfaces. Where might Alan have left his fingerprints? But she slowed and stopped. No, if the police came it would be foolish to deny that he had been there. Someone might have told the police he'd come—not Florian, he wouldn't betray her, but Tommy or one of Allan's friends? Anyone might know. She mustn't deny his visit, mustn't be caught out in a lie. Yes, Alan had called here—he was an old school friend. No, he didn't stay long. No, we weren't close friends, officer.

Really, miss—then what about this ring?

She wore her raincoat, the plastic hood up against the soft falling rain. Like Red Riding Hood, she thought, alone on an errand in the dark dangerous wood, hoping against hope she wouldn't meet the wolf. She kept her hands deep in the pouch-like pockets of her plastic raincoat, the fingers of her left hand resting lightly against the bones of Alan's finger and his ring. She must get rid of them quickly—they were evi-

dence. Where was best to dispose of them? Either side of the
street was lined with drab little houses, some with one remaining light on, the rest dark, their occupants asleep. Where
the gardens met the pavement were wire fences, hedges, plots
of land. Tidy gardens, untidy gardens, dog runs, lawns, concrete parking spaces. No rubbish bins. Hedges, flower gardens—she could bury the pieces separately, one piece in this
garden, one in that. Scraps of finger bone—no one would notice them in the ground. Even the keen gardener, digging over
his patch, uncovering a piece of bone among pebbles and grit
and chips of root, would think it just another little piece of
stone. And if they recognised it, a piece of bone, they'd never
think human—something a fox brought by, they'd think, a
piece of chicken. No, not chicken—people knew what
chicken bones looked like. They'd know it hadn't come from
chicken.

Lamb? Rabbit?

Best not to bury it. She had nothing to dig with anyway.
She should have brought the carving knife. Never mind—the
falling rain made the ground wet, so the earth should be soft
and muddy, and she ought to be able to dig into it with her
bare fingers. Make a hole, six inches, nine inches deep. Walk
away with dirty hands.

Evidence again.

Jo glanced along the street. About one house in four still
showed a light. Across the road a television flickered through
the curtain. People would be up. Not many—just the odd in-
somniac. Someone who couldn't sleep. Someone with
nothing better to do than stare dully from the window.

Watching her.

Keep it simple, she thought. If she took the pieces one by
one and tossed them singly into the bottoms of uncared-for
hedges she need hardly break her stride. Anyone watching

would hardly notice. Whoever owned the hedge would never root about in the leaves and rubbish. They'd never find a splinter of bone.

She began looking in the hedge bottoms as she walked. Despite the rain the loose leaves and scraps of paper seemed generally dry, protected by the hedges above. In the light of a streetlamp she stooped beside one to look more carefully. If she tossed a piece down, not here, not where the lamp glared brightly, but at the darkest midpoint between streetlamps, would it be out of sight? Or would it lie on top of the existing debris, gleaming fresh and new? She stood up, leaning briefly against the lamppost while a solitary car cruised slowly along the road towards her. She would wait until it passed.

It slowed. And stopped.

A police car.

Window winding down. Man leaning out. Lamp on top of the car extinguished. A girl and a police car beneath the streetlamp.

"You all right, miss?"

"Yes, thank you."

She took her hands out of her pockets. She'd show the police she wasn't carrying anything. Don't give them a reason to be suspicious.

"Late, isn't it?"

"I suppose so."

"It's raining. Not a good time for a walk."

"I couldn't sleep."

"On your own, then?"

She swallowed. "Yes."

"Just walking?"

"I stopped a moment."

"Beneath a lamp post. Nice and visible."

She frowned. What was he getting at? He peered at her. "Waiting for someone?"

"No, I'm . . ."

"What exactly?"

"Just having a walk."

She was breathing in shallow gasps. If he decided to search her—and he could, couldn't he, stop and search?—he'd look in her pockets, find the tiny bones. Find the ring: *To Alan, with Joanna's love.*

"Live locally?" he asked.

She nodded along the street. "I have a flat." Not for much longer. *I'm Getting Married in the Morning*: the stupid refrain ran through her head.

"Address?"

She told him, though each word seemed glued in her throat. *Ding, Dong, the Bells Are Gonna—*

"Name?"

She was exposed before him. He had her name, address, the precise time.

"What's under the coat?"

"My coat?"

His mouth twitched. It could have been a leer. "Are you dressed?"

"Of course."

"Didn't come out in a nightie—because you couldn't sleep?"

"I don't understand."

"Late at night. Raining. Woman standing beneath a lamp-post."

She realised now. She had been so concerned about the finger she hadn't realised how she might look. A common prostitute—that was what he thought. It seemed appropriate. No whore could be dirtier than her. She fiddled with the top button of her raincoat. "Do you want to see what I've got on? You've got the wrong idea."

"So would a lot of men." He stared at her. "Look, Miss . . . Beattie, is it? If you want my advice you'll go straight home. Make a cup of Horlicks." He grinned. "Want a lift out of the rain?"

"No," she said. "I prefer to walk."

"As you like," he said. "But don't beg any lifts from strangers."

She was in a side street. The police had gone.

She stared at the damp dark gardens without enthusiasm. She couldn't risk dumping the grisly evidence now the police had her name and address. But neither could she take the things home. She kept on walking.

She glanced in the gutter. Saw the obvious solution.

She closed her eyes briefly, her lashes damp with rain. Her face was wet and cold. She looked ahead, saw nothing, turned round. A dark, empty street. Long past midnight.

In one sudden movement Jo slipped her hand into her outside pocket, scrabbled for the scraps of bone, brought them out, peeped at them—saw the ring among them, her cheap teenage folly—darted across to the gutter and pushed the tiny pieces through the grill of the roadside drain. She stood up immediately.

Walked on.

All gone. All my sorrows, all forgotten. Yes, she thought as relief and happiness surged through her head: everything is done. Though the bones and ring had disappeared into the same soakaway drain they'd be washed away swiftly and go separate ways. In the gutter beside her feet black rainwater ran freely, flowing to the drain. All that water, she thought, draining underground. A flow of water. Carrying debris away.

So simple, she thought. Why didn't I think of it earlier? My brain had jammed. That was ridiculous. Childish. I must never let that happen again. From now on I must think clearly and decisively. Be forever calm.

She strode out along the shining pavement. The air was chilly and wet. But Jo didn't mind the wet. She could stand the wet—only the sunshine got her down.

Chapter 14

It had been a long, long morning. They were due at the church at four and it hadn't occurred to Jo that she would have most of the day entirely on her own, with nothing to do, no one to see, nothing to occupy her mind. It was a dead time, transitory, like the hours spent waiting at an airport before being whisked off in a plane. The old life left behind, the new life yet to begin. An unreal time.

She went for a walk, and later, back in her flat, she lay in a noontime hot bath, bubbles from the foam popping gently on her skin. She had poured a treble measure, because everything in the flat was disposable, part of the life she'd leave behind. She lay in the warm water and wondered how Miro had filled his morning, his last hours as a single man rattling around his empty house. He had probably gone into the office. Would Florian wait for him? Perhaps Miro had told him to collect him in an hour, two hours. In which case, Florian also had time on his hands. He might come round to see her. The thought made Jo shiver in the water. Florian couldn't do that—not on her wedding day. Imagine if he arrived now at the flat and found her relaxed in the water, warm and half asleep. Imagine that. Might he come? No, it was too dangerous. She moved her toe, gripped the chain, pulled the plug and stood up in the bath. As she dried herself she smelt of pine needles.

Dee came at two.

Jo was dressed by then and the first thing she noticed was that Dee's suit, which she would be wearing again after the ceremony, made Dee look overdressed. Over made-up. She was an attractive girl, had been a pretty child, but on special occasions she over-prepared. Today, for instance, Dee's clothes fit too tightly, the little jacket so snug that it squeezed her breasts like a Restoration corsage—though it must have been the bra that did that, two uplifting cups scooping her breasts and presenting them like overdone poached eggs. The blouse open to reveal freckles and cleavage. Her face immaculate, like painted china. Blonde hair lacquered into place. Dee would photograph beautifully but looked brittle to the touch.

Joanna checked herself in the mirror. Until Dee had come she had felt that her own slightly formal burgundy suit made a sensible going-away dress, but now it looked rigid and constrained. An interview suit. She should have chosen something more summery. But that might make her look too frivolous.

Dee asked, "Nervous?"

"I don't know."

"You'll be lady of the manor soon."

"Twin set and pearls."

They both giggled.

Dee went to where her white bridesmaid dress hung beside Jo's wedding gown. She touched the polythene. "It still doesn't like, seem real."

"Goodbye flat."

"Hello, manor house." Dee turned round. "Have you got a drink?"

"I'm not starting yet."

"Come on. You can't get married stone cold sober. I'm having one."

Jo went to the cupboard. "There's vodka."

141

"Excellent. Doesn't leave a smell. I'll get some ice."

Jo took out two glasses. "Just ice? Are you having it straight?"

"I'm easy. Anything."

Jo said, "I don't suppose one glass will hurt."

Dee reappeared with the ice. "Miro will have been on his stag night. Let's hope he isn't hung over."

"Too experienced for that."

Dee pulled a face. "Ah, the joys of older men."

They poured drinks. Jo said, "I'll tell you straight—sometimes I think I'd like a bit of youthful irresponsibility."

"Absolutely. Here's to young men—boys on the side. Swallow your drink!"

Dee downed hers in one and gasped. Jo laughed at her. "That was quick."

As Dee put down the empty glass she sneezed. "Wow! Too quick. Look at me." She sneezed again, began to laugh. "One glass and I'm a goner."

"It wasn't even a big one."

Dee giggled as she ran her finger round the inside of the glass. "What did you put in this?"

Jo sipped her own. "It did nothing for me."

"Have another. A woman's *supposed* to be light hearted on her wedding day."

"And sober."

"Who says?" Dee held out her glass. "One swig more."

Jo poured again, giving Dee the larger share. "You're not driving, at least."

"On a wedding day? You're joking. But I can carry my drink, you know—I have my duties to perform."

The doorbell rang.

"Oops," said Dee, putting down her glass. "That'll be your Mum."

"Oh, right," said Jo. She had thought it might be Florian.

At Electra Court, Florian put the finishing touches to the coffee tray, then carried it like a butler to the two men in Miro's study. "Ah, coffee," boomed Jasper. "Something in it, I hope?"

"Mustn't spoil Mr. Vermont's malt, sir."

"Plenty of time for that later," Miro said.

Florian and Jasper flicked their eyebrows. Jasper said, "You really ought to take something to set you up for church, Miro."

Florian was pouring coffee. "A chaser, sir?"

Jasper glanced at Miro, then said, "We'd better wait."

"Never too soon for a little one," purred Florian. "On an early morning shoot we always have a snifter before dawn. Something to brace us for the day."

The way they dither, he thought, you'd think they sus pect him of poisoning their drink. As if he would. As if he'd need to drug their whisky. Coffee was easier. They'll definitely drink that. And what could be more natural than that after they've drunk it, he flushes the dregs away down the drain?

Miro turned to Jasper, ignoring Florian. "What can we do about this bloody supermarket? One little flood. I mean, what did it cost them, really?"

"Insurance will pay."

"We don't need this publicity."

"Your coffee," said Florian, moving in.

Miro continued: "I wouldn't mind, but we've fixed it now. At our own expense."

Jasper took his coffee. Outside the window, he saw clouds scudding across the sun. "Funny weather. Hope it keeps fine."

"Sort of day you don't know what'll happen." Miro sipped his coffee. "Oh well. It can only get better."

Jasper laughed. "Come on, Miro, you're getting married. Happiest day of your life."

"Oh, don't mind me. I'm like the English weather," Miro muttered. "Whatever I was like this morning I'll be different this afternoon."

Florian deliberately poured himself a cup. They hadn't noticed he'd placed a third cup on the tray—but why shouldn't he join them? It was a special day, a celebration. Florian smiled. Miro might be marrying her but, though he didn't know it, he was already sharing his wife to be. That was something he knew and Miro didn't. But better than that: once today was over, Jo would be living in Electra Court. Just the three of them. And when Miro was at work, there'd be just the two of them. While Miro was erecting buildings, Florian would—

He laughed aloud.

When Joanna's Mum arrived, the sun went in. A brief squall of rain rattled against the windows and her mother's first action was to switch on the light. She took off her coat and shook it as if she'd been caught in the rain. "That was lucky," she said. "Thought I was for it. Didn't like that taxi, mind. Had the window down."

Jo took her coat.

As she hung it up, her mother moved smartly around the room making sure the windows were shut. She sniffed. "Could do with some air in here. Smells like a tart's boudoir."

"Open a window."

"And let in the rain?"

She was smaller than Jo, her dark hair pulled back and

pinned like a flamenco dancer, her eyes black as jet. She wore an orange suit.

"Morning, Dee. You look a million dollars." She turned to Jo. "I don't like that dress. You didn't ought to wear red."

"It's burgundy."

"Thought it was wool. It does nothing for you." She glanced at the side table and the two vodka glasses. "Feeling nervous, are we?"

"My idea," said Dee.

"You know what's best, I'm sure."

She ran her finger across the nearest wooden surface and peered at the smudge on her skin. "You'll have to do better than that in his lordship's house."

"I'll make some coffee," said Jo.

"Don't I get a gin?"

Dee collected the glasses. "It was vodka," she said.

"Vodka? I don't hold with that."

"Vodka or nothing," said Jo.

"Coffee then."

Her mother dropped in an armchair and bounced on the cushion. Because her feet didn't reach the ground, she jiggled on the cushion like a spoilt child on a horse. "And not too much milk," she said.

Jo went to the kitchen. "How many sugars?" she called.

"Forgotten, have you? Of course, you don't never come home."

"One," said Jo.

"And a bit," said her Mum. She was looking round the room like a prospective tenant. "You'll be glad to see the back of this place."

"I like it," called Jo. "I'm thinking of keeping it on."

"Oh yes," sniffed her mother. "I bet. Like when a millionaire says he still likes fish and chips out of newspaper.

Likes to slum it now and then."

"Have you seen the new house?" Dee asked pleasantly.

"It's very nice, I'm sure, if you like that sort of thing."

"Did *you* like it?"

Mrs. Beattie snorted. "Haven't seen it, have I? I'll tell you when I have. 'Cos I'll be lucky if I get another invite." She dropped her voice to a loud stage whisper: "I was only asked because she *has* to have her mother to her wedding. *His* idea, I bet. Otherwise it wouldn't have looked right."

"No," said Dee. "She wants you there."

"You don't understand, Dee love. You always kept in touch with *your* mother."

Jo appeared with a coffee. "I keep in touch with you."

"High days and special occasions."

Jo gave her the coffee. "Another vodka?" she asked Dee.

Her mother rattled her coffee. "Gawd! You'll both be tipsy."

"We're inseparable," said Dee.

Mrs. Beattie sniffed suspiciously at her coffee. "Come on, then. Let's have a look at this precious wedding dress. I dread to think."

"Time for a whisky," Miro said.

He and Jasper had moved into Miro's vast living room, a room cleaned and tidied, nothing out of place, its flat surfaces cleared of ornaments, the polished air heavy with expectancy. Guests would mingle here. They would bring mud in on their shoes, leave rings beneath their glasses, drop sandwiches. One or two would smoke. Miro had moved his Afghan rug upstairs.

He poured two glasses of his favourite malt, smiled at Jasper, then replaced the bottle out of sight, deep inside his drinks cabinet. They raised their glasses in a toast. Both men were dressed in the smart business suits they would wear throughout the day—Miro felt morning suits were pretentious. He wore a dicky bow and Jasper sported a conventionally shaped but vivid tie. Both men had handkerchiefs in their breast pockets.

They were alone in the living room. Florian had gone off in the car, and a small band of catering staff were toiling in the kitchen. Miro looked nervous, Jasper thought.

"Any easier the second time?" he asked.

"Less trouble. With Isabel it was rather a grand affair—the full church ceremony, hotel reception, a ceilidh with far too many guests. Still, her father paid."

"But you're paying for this?"

"Of course. Jo's family has no money." He swallowed his malt. "There's only her mother. You know."

"She all right?"

Miro raised his eyebrows meaningfully. "They're not close, so we won't see much of her."

Miro turned his back to the room and stared morosely at his garden. "It does work, you know. Jo's not interested in pop music and clubbing. Quite a mature girl, in her way."

"I bet."

"She's got an older mind."

"Some girls do have." Jasper walked to join him at the window. The garden outside was damp but the sun had appeared again. "Most girls are silly and although you fancy them like hell they never look at an older man, so nothing comes of it. But some girls are attracted to . . . the more mature man. We're allowed to try."

"The world is full of pretty women."

Outside the window, insects were at work again, butterflies flittering from flower to flower.

Jasper asked, "You're not worried, are you, Miro?"

"Marriage is a lifetime commitment."

Jasper pulled a mock sombre face. "Commitment's the word—a lifetime, and that's a damn long time."

Miro nudged him. "At least if I marry a young girl I won't go chasing them any more—unlike some people."

Jasper chuckled. "Make her pregnant as soon as possible."

"Take away her youthful bloom?"

"Seriously, if the girl stays young and unencumbered and you get older by the year, what do you think is going to happen? Give her a reason to stay with you."

"I want kids, Jasper."

"I never did. They just happened, you know? Ballast weighing down the marriage." Jasper laughed shortly and moved away. "Oh, I play around a little—it doesn't mean anything. Drink up. We shouldn't be talking like this on your wedding day."

Miro was still staring out the window. "It does no harm to be serious once in a while. It's a serious day." He turned. "But you're right. I'll make Jo pregnant—and we'll raise a family together. Kids will be the foundation of our life."

Jasper grinned uneasily. "Time for another drink, I think."

"Don't forget you'll be driving. No, I've no doubts about marrying Jo. I know she's young, but I love her." He chuckled bashfully. "I deserve her, don't I?"

When the doorbell rang Mrs. Beattie said, "That'll be flowers, I bet. You haven't got many here. This place should be full of flowers."

"They'd only be wasted," said Jo, studying her reflection in the mirror. She had the wedding dress on now, a cloud of white. "I'm not coming back here. They'd only wither and die."

"I could've had 'em."

"Will you answer that door? Dee and I can't, dressed like this."

"I wouldn't say no to a bunch of flowers," said Mrs. Beattie as she stood up. "Not that anyone ever buys *me* flowers."

She strutted to the door as Dee emerged from the bathroom, the white bridesmaid dress loose about her shoulders. "I never could get into this. I said it was too tight."

Dee stood with her back to Jo to let her tug at the fastenings on the back. Jo said, "You can't have put on weight, Dee. You don't weigh anything as it is."

Mrs. Beattie reappeared, her face tight with disapproval. "It's him," she said.

Florian had to squeeze past her to get in the room. He had two posies of flowers.

Dee said, "You can't come in here—we're dressing."

Florian grinned. "Looks like I missed the exciting bit. You both look lovely."

Mrs. Beattie said, "Shouldn't the driver wait in the car?"

"We're ready," snapped Jo. "Well, how do we look?"

Mrs. Beattie studied her critically, but Jo was looking at Florian. He ignored her and said, "Tell you the truth, Dee, I've never seen you look so beautiful."

Dee coloured and moved away. "I haven't done my hair yet."

"You could have fooled me."

"How about the bride?" asked Jo, staring at him. "Don't I look beautiful?"

Florian turned back to her, looking her up and down as professionally as a couturier. "Magnificent." He paused. "I could almost marry you myself."

To lighten his words he grinned at the other two. But Jo

whispered, "Do I really look nice?"

He smiled at her and said, "Good enough to eat."

Jo may have made little impression on the neighbourhood, but in leaving she caused a stir. The smart Lexus had been seen before—even the chauffeur had been marked—but the emergence of two young women in wedding dresses could not pass unnoticed. Children and old ladies stared in the street, neighbours came to their windows, and a dog appeared from somewhere to run yapping around their feet. Fitting Dee and Jo into the car was like cramming a suitcase with balloons— one look at the rear door and their flouncy white dresses seemed to inflate. Florian had to squeeze the material against their legs to get it through the door arch. He pushed Dee inside first and when he eased Jo in after her he had one arm round her back, one on her legs, and it seemed necessary for him to practically lift Jo inside like a precious parcel. Jo stumbled slightly, slipped a hand on Florian's shoulder, and as he helped her into her seat he leant right into the car and for one brief moment—unnoticed by anyone else—his head brushed against her white organza bosom.

Mrs. Beattie stood on the pavement like a passer-by whose way was blocked. To protect her orange suit against any passing shower of rain she carried a white mac and a collapsible umbrella. Her handbag was white also, and too large. Her shoes were white to match. She waited, kicking her painful feet. When Florian had fitted his charges into the rear Mrs. Beattie was still at the front passenger door waiting for the serving man to open it. But he didn't seem to notice. He walked round the car into the street, got in and switched on the ignition. Then he leant across to release the door. She glared at Jo's neighbours and got inside.

As they pulled away, Florian said, "This is your big day."

"Here comes the bride," laughed Dee.

Mrs. Beattie sniffed.

As the first guests arrived at the church there was a sudden short burst of rain, a tiny dark cloud wandering alone across the sky and shedding its burden on those below. People already out of their cars ran for shelter in the little village church. Those arriving stayed inside their vehicles until the brief shower had passed. Jasper was in the vestibule, his confident large frame filling the cramped space as he welcomed arriving guests and showed them where to go. Since practically all the guests were Miro's they had decided not to divide the interior of the church into bride and bridegroom's sides but to put everyone together according to a complicated system of Miro's own. Jasper had never understood Miro's logic, but he'd reprinted the names alphabetically, and with avuncular authority he directed the guests to their designated pews.

The little church had been built in the first decade of the eighteenth century of local Cotswold stone whose original honey colour turned grey each passing winter. In places it was lost behind dark ivy. Inside the church, the walls were plastered and cream painted, with tablets inset into them bearing the names and deeds of local benefactors and long-dead landowners. One window was a blaze of Victorian stained glass, bringing colour and vibrancy to the quiet interior. Light streamed in from all the leaded windows onto the dust of the stone-flagged floor and across the old wooden pews. For the ceremony today the altar had been laid with a freshly laundered cloth of white and green, with several pieces of polished brass along the top. They shone like gold.

The vicar for this and several other local churches was a slightly built, wispy haired man approaching retirement, called Ellis Jones. He enjoyed weddings and christenings and Harvest Festival and anything that warmed a neglected church with unaccustomed crowds, and today he beamed on the gathering visitors as if they might be persuaded to come again. He mothered the anxious Miro like an actor before a show.

"A wonderful day," sighed Ellis. "The last clouds have blown away. Quite perfect. Well, Mr. Vermont, now that nearly everyone's inside, perhaps you'd like to come in and wait for your lovely young bride."

Chapter 15

It felt as if a bright spotlight shone through the Victorian stained-glass window straight down into the aisle to pick her out. The brightness warmed her and she felt a rush of happiness, a shy confidence, a desire to sing along with the music resounding through the church. Though she seemed to be walking in slow motion, the faces around her were blurred. Yet they seemed to emanate good will. Even her mother waddling beside her, clutching her arm too hard, seemed maternal. Dee, unseen behind her, was her best friend. Organ music soared. There was a smell of candle wax and flowers. Ahead at the altar stood Miro, his reassuring broad back towards her, and beyond him stood the white-haired and white-robed vicar, facing her, welcoming her to the ceremony. Her ceremony.

There was a step up before the altar, and she almost tripped. Then she was standing beside Miro. Her husband. Almost. When they glanced at each other her tight, anxious smile was met by his relaxed, encouraging grin. The vicar was saying something. The words were so familiar that she thought for a moment he was talking only to her.

"Dearly beloved, we are gathered together here in the sight of God and in the face of this congregation to join together this man and this woman in holy matrimony . . ."

The pounding of her blood subsided and a joyful calm

floated down. The sense of impossible unreality was replaced by a sharp awareness of exactly where she was, who she was with, what was about to happen. When she relaxed her shoulders she heard the rustling of her dress. In the scent of flowers she could smell a mingled bouquet of other women's perfumes. She heard the shuffling of people's feet. Someone dropped a book. There was a slight draught, as if the door had been left open, a sound as if one or two latecomers were still coming in.

"—for the procreation of children, to be brought up in the fear and nurture of the Lord, and to the praise of His holy name."

Miro wants children, she thought.

"—for a remedy against sin, and to avoid fornication . . ."

He stood solid and comfortable beside her. She would be true to him.

"—into which holy estate these two persons present come now to be joined. Therefore if any man can show just cause why they may not lawfully be joined together, let him now speak, or else hereafter for ever hold his peace."

Ellis Jones smiled at her and looked out into the church.

A man shouted.

Ellis twitched. Jo felt the warmth leave her face.

The man shouted again but his words were lost in the startled gasps around the church. Ellis looked out beyond her. Miro turned round. Jo stood momentarily paralysed. She didn't want to turn round, to stare into the faces of all those people watching. But the man called out again, and when she turned around to face him she found that no one in the congregation was watching her at all. They were shuffling about in the pews, craning their necks to see who was causing the disturbance at the back. But she could see.

When she saw who it was she took an involuntary step towards him but for the first time realised that Miro had a firm grip on her arm. He muttered something. She wasn't listening. She was concentrating on the angry young man standing at the back of the church, in the centre of the aisle. She could see his face so clearly it was as if he stood only a few feet away. She could see his eyes—the fear in them, and the determination to make his voice heard. She knew that he stayed at the back of the church because he didn't dare come farther in. And in her icy paralysis Jo understood his caution. He was afraid that if he came into the body of the church, into the crowd of Miro's friends, he might be swallowed up. He was a stranger here.

They stood at opposite ends of the central aisle, both bodies rigid as they stared into each other's eyes. No one else in the aisle. The entire congregation penned in their wooden pews while he stood at the back of the aisle like Moses dividing the Red Sea.

Then Tommy said, "She can't marry him. She's engaged to my brother."

Ellis Jones asked the congregation to remain seated. He explained that it was his duty to establish whether there was any reason the marriage should not proceed. He called Tommy forward and after a slight hesitation the intruder walked self-consciously down the aisle. Everyone's eyes were upon him. He was a well-built man in his mid twenties, with his dead brother's colouring and sandy hair. He even walked like Alan, if they could have known. But no one knew his brother, except Florian and Jo. She couldn't look at Tommy, and she wouldn't look around the church for Florian, so she stared at the stone floor. In an earlier age she could have fainted, but here, mercilessly exposed in her wedding dress, she had to stand and face him as he approached. She felt condemned again, on the gallows platform, waiting for the trap to open beneath her feet. Then Miro took her hand and squeezed it, and the comfort of his touch almost made Joanna cry. She looked up and found Tommy a few feet in front of her. He was staring at her, but she looked away.

As the grave-faced vicar led the main players into the vestry, the hiss of whispers from the congregation erupted into a buzz of incredulous debate. Everyone had questions, but no one had answers. Someone cracked a joke. Nobody laughed.

In the tiny vestry it was so crowded they were practically rubbing against each other. Miro's face was red and he had to be forcibly held back by Jasper. Ellis Jones manoeuvred himself between Tommy and the others, and to regain control he spoke in the unnaturally loud voice he used in church.

"Young man, please listen to what I have to say. If you know of any impediment why these two may not be coupled together in matrimony, either by God's law or the law of the realm, I must ask you to prove your allegation—"

"She's engaged already—"

"—or you must supply sufficient evidence as would give good cause to defer this solemnisation until such time as the truth can be tried."

"Truth!" This was Miro.

"What is your name?" asked Ellis Jones.

"Ask *her!*" spat Tommy.

"Do you know this man, Jo?"

"Yes, he's called Thomas Pirie. But there's absolutely—"

"I think it better," Ellis interrupted, "if I speak to Mr. . . . Pirie on my own."

"You surely don't believe the man?" snapped Miro.

"I have to hear his case. Look, I'm afraid there isn't room for all of us in here."

"I demand to hear every word he says."

Ellis looked pained. "It would be easier—"

"Where's my brother?" Tommy asked.

They glared at him. "Well, if *you* don't know . . ." said Jasper with a smile.

"He came to your house," said Tommy. "Didn't he? He came to see you."

"Hardly makes him engaged to her," purred Jasper.

"He is. *She* is. They're engaged."

"*Did* you see his brother?" asked Miro.

She hardly hesitated at all. "Yes. Once. He was a school friend, that's all. We had nothing to say to each other."

"You didn't tell me."

Tommy snarled, "She wouldn't, would she?"

"Nothing happened. It wasn't important."

"But you didn't . . ." Miro faltered.

Jasper said, "She's quite right, Miro—it isn't important. Even if something did happen, which I'm sure it didn't—no, listen, Miro—whether they saw each other, whether he came to the house, is beside the point." He looked at Tommy. "You say they're engaged to marry?"

"Yeah."

"We're not—"

"If they're engaged to marry," Jasper asked, "how come we've never heard of him? Was it a *secret* engagement?"

"Been engaged for ages."

"Joanna?"

She shook her head. "No, honestly, this is completely untrue. I don't know why he's saying this."

"Mr. Pirie?"

"What?"

"Do you have evidence? A ring perhaps?"

"One moment," said Ellis firmly. "Whether or not there

157

was an engagement between these two young people—"

"There wasn't!" she cried.

"Either way," he continued, "there is clearly no engagement now. For all we know, Miss Beattie may have called it off—"

"I didn't. There wasn't one—"

"Liar!"

"Enough!" roared Miro. "I won't stand for this. Jo, once and for all, have you ever—oh God—have you ever been engaged to this man's brother?"

"No."

"Come on, Ellis, this is stupid. Let's get on with the service."

"It's not quite as easy—"

Miro cut him off. "If Jo *was* engaged before—which she wasn't—then the only person that could possibly affect is *me*. But she wasn't engaged—and not even this madman claims that she is *married* to his brother. So she's single, she's free to marry, and she is marrying *me*. Now!"

He made to pull Jo from the room, but Tommy suddenly lurched around Ellis and grabbed her by the arm. "Where's my brother?"

She tried to free herself. Jasper tugged Tommy's arm. "Calm down. You're sweating. You won't find him here."

"Why not? This is the last place he come to when he disappeared. You've done something to him."

"Done something?"

"He come here, didn't he, then disappeared?"

"He's mad!" cried Jo.

"You're marrying quick so you can cover up what happened."

Jasper forced himself between Tommy and the frightened

girl. "That's quite enough, young man. You're making yourself ridiculous."

"Where is he?"

"Excuse me." A new voice: Florian's head appeared round the door. "People are worried out there. Is there anything I can tell them?"

"We'll be out in a minute," Miro snapped.

Jasper said, "I'd better speak to them all. Best man and all that. Look, will someone hold onto this young fool?"

"Be glad to," said Florian, sliding into the crowded room.

Jasper looked at the vicar: "Ellis, there's no—impediment now, is there? No reason not to continue with the service?"

"No!" howled Tommy.

Florian had hold of him. "Silence," he hissed.

Ellis sniffed. "As I understand it, the sum total of this young man's claim is that Miss Beattie was supposedly engaged some time before?"

"My brother!"

"She wasn't," growled Miro, as Jasper pushed by to the door.

"Let me make this clear," said Ellis. "Even if she *was* engaged before, she does not consider herself engaged to him now. And in the ceremony we are about to resume—"

"*Resume.* Good," said Jasper at the door.

"—Miss Beattie will finally and irrevocably 'forsake all others' in front of everyone present. I assume, Miss Beattie, that you will be willing to make that vow?"

"Of course."

"Exactly," said Jasper. "She forsakes all others. I'll tell everyone to settle down. What d'you think, vicar—shall we start again from the top?"

Ellis waved a hand. "I'll pick it up."

Jasper disappeared.

Tommy shouted at Miro: "You've done something, I know it. You'll be sorry you married her."

Ellis was gentle. "That's enough of that, young man."

"Indeed!" said Florian airily. "Off you go, everyone, I'll look after Mr. Pirie, don't you mind."

Tommy tried to wrench away but Florian was too strong. The vicar touched Florian's arm. "You will remember we're in a church?"

"Peace and love, sir." Ellis stared at him. "He'll calm down when we're alone."

Ellis exhaled. Ignoring Miro's impatience he spoke in measured tones to Tommy. "You clearly have troubles, and I'm sorry for you. If you'd like to discuss things with me later . . ." Tommy clenched his teeth. Ellis said, "I am truly sorry you're in such pain."

He stepped back, smiled at Tommy, then led Miro and Jo back into the church.

Florian kept his grip on Tommy, who said nothing but continued to glare at the vestry door. They were alone. "So you're in pain, are you?" murmured Florian.

Tommy muttered, "You knew my name."

"Mhm?"

"Just now, you called me Mr. Pirie. How'd you know my name?"

"You're famous, I think."

"Not when I come in here. No one knew me from bleeding Adam."

"Not even from bleeding *Alan*," quipped Florian.

"You know about it, don't you?"

Suddenly, Tommy flicked his head sideways, trying to butt Florian in the face. But he wasn't well placed, and Florian slammed a punch low in his belly. As Tommy sagged, Florian grabbed his head and brought it down to meet his own rising knee. Tommy fell coughing to the vestry floor.

"Oh look," said Florian. "You've started bleeding. What'll people say?"

As Tommy struggled to his feet Florian hit him hard on the back of the neck. Tommy crumpled and began groaning on the floor. "They'll say I didn't look after you."

Tommy tried to speak. Florian knelt beside him to hear Tommy's words: "You know . . . what happened . . . to Alan. You know . . . what them bastards did."

"Tell me."

Florian grinned contentedly around the poky vestry. There was a small pile of out-of-date hymn books, some kneelers, a furled banner and a pair of religious framed prints on the wall. The room smelt of clerical dust.

Tommy spoke with difficulty. "I think they . . . killed him."

Florian chuckled. "That's a bit far fetched."

"Alan told me . . . they wouldn't want him. So I reckon they . . . got rid of him."

"My boss did? Oh, I couldn't believe that."

Florian patted him on the head, got up, and peeped out of the vestry door. He wondered whether there might be another exit from the church.

Tommy spluttered, "But they wouldn't want you to know about it . . . would they?"

Florian knelt beside him again. "I won't hear ill of my boss, Thomas. I'm a trusting kind of man. In fact, I'm so charitable, I don't believe *anyone's* worse than me."

Chapter 16

Miro was so busy accepting congratulations he didn't have time to look for Florian. But to travel the short distance from the little church to Electra Court, most people used their cars, if only to have them re-parked more conveniently. In Miro's Lexus, which went first, he and Jo were alone for practically the first time in the day. Miro drove because Florian had disappeared somewhere. Miro didn't seem concerned.

"Was it terrible for you?" he asked.

"Like a dream." She shook her head. "The bad and the good parts all mixed up. Why would he say those things?"

"It's over now," said Miro, his hand dropping to her thigh. "He's disappeared."

"I knew his brother—years ago. But we were never engaged."

"It's all right, darling. You're allowed to have previous boyfriends. As long as they *are* previous!"

They were at his gate, left open to receive the guests. As they swept along the drive she noticed that the fountain was on full power, frothing a welcome. A damp sun shone on the house. The head of the catering staff stood on the steps like a butler, but Miro merely waved an acknowledgement and continued round the back to the garages beside the annex. He eased the car into its slot. Jo opened her door, but when she got out she found that there was too little room between the garage wall and the car for the unusual width of her white wedding dress. She clutched it to her as she closed the Lexus door, then she inched between the car and the wall to the cobbled courtyard.

Miro was waiting there. He said, "You've got a smudge on your dress."

She peered down at it in dismay. Looking up, she saw Florian step into the yard from the glass door leading to the annex. She felt unclean. She muttered, "I'm going inside to change," and hurried away across the courtyard. But Florian said, "Don't you want to hear about Mr. Pirie?"

"Oh—Thomas." She felt foolish. A smudge of dirt on her wedding dress was enough to make her forget all about Alan's brother. Miro asked where Thomas was.

"In the annex."

"*Here?* Can't we get rid of him?"

Florian grinned wickedly, but Miro shook his head. "No, be serious. Can't you take him away? This is a wedding reception. We can't have that madman here."

"He won't be."

Miro stared at him. Florian said, "Go ahead and have the party. I'll look after him."

Jo said, "Guests are arriving. Can't you hear the cars? I'll leave you to sort it out."

Miro spun on her. "How d'you expect us to sort it out? We can't just leave him in the annex."

Florian said, "He won't get out. You get changed, Jo."

Miro stopped her. "What's going on? You two don't seem to realise how serious this is."

"He can't escape," said Florian.

"Take him back to town."

Florian frowned at him, looking almost disappointed. "You wouldn't want Thomas talking to the police, would you—or the press? We can't have scandal."

"I'm going in," Jo said.

"That's right, your guests will be waiting," agreed Florian. "They'll wonder where you are." He smiled at Miro. "Enjoy the party. Behave as if nothing had happened. We can talk about Thomas when everyone's gone home."

Jo turned and ran to the kitchen door. Miro looked distracted: "What'll we do about him?"

"It's not your problem."

Miro frowned.

"You're the groom, the main attraction. Go and entertain your guests—help them forget this ever happened."

"But if someone asks?"

"Tell them the madman has gone home."

Miro stared, uncomprehending. He could hear car doors slamming in front of the house. He said, "All right, Florian. Do as you think best."

One thing that running Vermont Era had taught Miro was how to put on a brave face. As he circulated among his guests he looked the proud and confident new husband. He and Jasper were like British businessmen on an export drive, finely dressed, well spoken and assured. The catering staff drifted among chatting guests and offered canapés and champagne. Soft music played, lost beneath the bubble of conversation, the tinkle of glasses, the popping of champagne corks.

Miro paid no attention. Behind his reassuring smile his thoughts skittered between the interrupted ceremony, his wife's admission that she knew the man, the conversation they must have later—and the presence of the wretched Thomas in the annex across the courtyard. He hardly noticed who he spoke to; each was greeted with the same bonhomie. He didn't notice Jo's mother already quaffing her third glass of champagne, nor the vicar at her elbow gently trying to slow the woman down. Those two could be stuck with each other—a pair who didn't fit the general milieu of the party. Outsiders at the feast, invited on sufferance, their duties done.

Dee was out of her bridesmaid's dress and in scanty underclothes when Joanna came through the bedroom door. But at the sound of the door opening Dee turned as calmly as if fully dressed.

"That's a shame," she laughed. "Could've been a chunky man."

Dee slipped into her tight little raspberry jacket—nothing between it and her bra—then reached for her black skirt. Jo wandered across the bedroom to look down from the window at the drive packed with parked cars, the rose beds, the lawns, the fountain spurting in the air. The sun was shining and a few white clouds sailed across a bright blue sky. Dee chattered on: "It's a shame you have to get out of your lovely wedding dress."

"I've got a mark on it."

"I'm going to have mine altered—it's far too good to waste. I'll probably drag it out again for Christmas!"

Jo stayed at the mullion window. In the white organza dress she looked like a bride from the nineteenth century. Behind her, Dee had wriggled into her skirt. She skipped barefoot across the room to join Jo at the window. "A married woman."

"No going back."

"Feel different?"

Jo shook her head. "It's like a birthday—it may *be* different but it doesn't feel different."

Dee said, "This afternoon you were Joanna Beattie. You're Mrs. Vermont now."

"Don't know who I am at the moment."

"It's an unreal day," Dee said airily. "The wedding dress marks a kind of bridge—something you wear while you change from one side to the other."

Jo chuckled uneasily. "Perhaps that's why I don't want to take it off."

Dee found her shoes and pulled them on. She glanced at her dress flung on the bed but decided to leave it there. When she went to the door she blew Jo a kiss.

"Enjoy your day," she said, and left.

Dee didn't see Florian at the far end of the upper landing: she wasn't meant to. He waited till she had turned the corner, then he stepped out from the spare bedroom doorway and slipped quickly to his master's room. He didn't knock.

Jo gave a slight start at the window. "You shouldn't be here."

Florian turned the key in the old lock.

"What are you doing?" Jo asked.

"What does a bride want on her wedding day?"

He was across the room, reaching out his hand. "Come away from the window."

"You can't—not now."

He took her hand. "When better?"

"We can't do it here."

He pulled her towards the bed, saying, "This is the bridal chamber," and he placed his hand on Joanna's breast. She put her hand on Florian's, but she didn't try to push him away. Anyone coming in would have thought her small pink hand was pressing Florian's fingers to her organza bosom.

"Not here, please, Florian."

"I waited till Dee left."

"I have to change now."

He pushed her down onto the bed. She tried to speak but

he closed her mouth with a savage kiss. She struggled free. "Not like this."

"No time for foreplay."

He slid his fingers inside her bodice, and she felt his hand gently clasp her breast. He rubbed her nipple. She said, "Someone will come."

"No, this is your private room." He was panting now, his other hand sliding down her thigh.

She said, "Miro—"

"Busy. Downstairs."

Florian pushed his hand into the layers of lace beneath her skirt.

"No," she said. "You'll ruin the dress."

His hand reached Jo's panties. She kept her legs closed. He gripped her breast.

"I could rip this sweet dress off you."

"Let me take it off."

He laughed, close to her face, before he kissed her again roughly. As she lay beneath him she felt his hand leave her breast and pull at the flimsy shoulder strap.

"I'll undo it," she said. "Don't tear my dress."

He slid the strap off her shoulder and when he pulled it further her breast lazily popped out. Leisurely, he kissed the soft smooth pink-white flesh. His other hand was inside her panties. But Jo knew he wasn't fingering her there to pleasure her, he only touched her because he could. She felt his fingers slide inside her—but not roughly; he could be gentle when he wanted to be. He stroked her softly and she sobbed, once. Florian was feeling if she was wet.

"I must take my dress off."

"Don't you realise, Jo? I want you *in* the dress. I want the bride."

"You'll spoil it."

167

"I want to rip it apart. I want to rip into you."

But for all his rough words Florian treated the white dress like something precious. He had both her breasts exposed now and he was free to push her skirts up along her legs. The soft bundle of organza and creamy lace lay across her tummy and Florian buried his face in the bridal material while he pulled off her pretty panties. Then he lowered his face. She felt his tongue.

"No," she whispered. "You mustn't."

But he did.

His hands reached for her breasts again and she couldn't resist him. As Florian licked her, it seemed to Jo she must be running with warm liquid. "You'll ruin the wedding dress," she whimpered.

He paused. She gasped—she didn't want Florian to stop. He said, "You care more about the dress than anything."

"You'll stain it."

"Not yet I won't."

Under her backside was the crumpled material of the bridesmaid's dress, from where Dee had flung it on the bed. But Jo didn't tell him. She didn't want to talk to Florian. She wanted—

Florian was shifting. He swung his body across her, moved his face up along her body to nuzzle her breasts and then, in one seamless movement he entered her. He was huge, hot and swollen—yet for the first time she swallowed him easily. For the first time, she didn't fear that he might tear her apart. She could hold him, squeeze him, push back, match his urgent movements with strong thrusts of her own. But he wasn't waiting. He thumped and crashed against her, ploughing inside as deep as he could go. She threshed on the bed, trapped and tangled in her wedding gown, grinding Dee's white dress beneath her into Miro's crumpled bed clothes. And when Florian shuddered, stopped and slumped against her, Jo laughed and gazed wide-eyed at the bedroom ceiling. Florian seemed to have fallen asleep. But she was awake.

Miro had gone outside to the garden because he thought that if he made one more circuit of the ground floor reception rooms, one more round of pleasantries with the guests, his mask would slip and he would scream. What was he celebrating? His wedding had been ruined by some raving idiot who, no matter how much he tried to dismiss the man's allegations, was the brother of Jo's ex-boyfriend. An ex-boyfriend who, unknown to Miro, had been to the house. As she hadn't denied—but as she hadn't told him, either. And where was she now? Upstairs presumably, with a "headache" or one of the other "female problems," which girls never seemed to be troubled with till they married and which afterwards seldom left them. Why was it that her first action after the marriage ceremony was to go upstairs and take to bed?

Miro walked the length of his lawn, through the open gate and peered outside. The air seemed calmer there. As he gazed along the quiet lane he pondered the wisdom of having such a young wife. He glanced up at his bedroom window. No one there, of course. At least she hadn't closed the curtains; she wasn't lying on the bed having a full scale migraine or a sulk. But presumably she was in there. So perhaps he should go up to the bedroom and see how she was. She might be waiting for him to place a cool hand on her fevered brow.

At the foot of the stairs he met Florian coming down. Before Miro could think anything of it Florian said, "Glad to see you, sir. I've been looking for you everywhere."

"A problem?"

"Oh, not at all. Everything's rosy, sir."

"Then what . . ."

Miro glanced at the various guests milling in the hall. Florian caught the glance, and stepped closer. "Not the best place, sir. Perhaps we should—"

Miro sighed. "Out in the garden, then. Come on."

As Florian followed Miro through aimless guests he had a half smile on his face. Miro selected an unoccupied section of lawn, and Florian said, "The roses look particularly fine this year."

"Yes—"

"Come out in celebration, one might say."

"This Thomas character."

"Sir?"

"Where is he?"

Florian caught the blaze in Miro's eye, so answered soberly: "The man is gone, sir."

"Gone? You said he couldn't escape."

"I didn't say he had."

Miro's eyes narrowed, but Florian continued smoothly, "I thought it best to let him go. He had calmed down considerably."

Miro looked across the lawn. It was early evening now and a chill had crept into the air. He chewed his lip. "I hope he won't make trouble."

"I doubt it."

Miro stared at him, but Florian's face showed nothing. Except—

"What's that lipstick on your face, Florian?"

"Lipstick?" Florian's hand flew to his cheek. "No, it was washed since."

"Since when, man?"

Florian grinned. "Since a while back. One of the catering girls . . ."

Miro sighed.

Miro was no sooner back in the house when Jasper grabbed his arm. "Miro! You're neglecting your friends shamefully. Come inside and have a drink."

"I've done nothing but drink all day."

"Rubbish. I've hardly seen you with a glass in your hand since we came back. Don't tell me marriage has made a changed man of you already?"

"Marriage!" Miro shook his head.

"Early days," laughed Jasper, dragging the reluctant Miro into the drawing room crowded with guests. "My wife wants to congratulate you."

"You just want to dump her on me."

"Oh! Such a cynic about marriage already."

But on their way across the room, Dee stepped into their path. She was slightly tipsy—not unattractively so: her cheeks were flushed, her eyes sparkled, and her smile was wicked. She asked, "When does the dancing start?"

"Not yet," said Miro. "Have you seen Jo?"

"Yes, but we *must* have dancing, Miro. Now!" She laughed. "You could burst me with a pin—so much sin I'm holding in."

"I'll talk to someone about it—"

"*Tell* them, Miro. You're in charge." Dee placed her hand on Jasper's arm. "And we can't wait, can we, Jasper?"

He didn't *quite* step back from her. "I was taking Miro across to my *wife*."

She bobbed her head. "Well, while Miro's talking to her . . ."

"Sorry, Dee. I'll talk to you later."

"Maybe, if you're lucky."

She watched for a moment, then began looking for someone lively.

On this occasion, Florian knocked. But when she called "Who is it?" he went straight in and found her lying on the bed, her white dress awry, the bed a mess of tangled linen. The sun had moved, and though it was not dark yet it was almost time to switch on a lamp. Florian closed the door.

"Miro's looking for you."

"He would be."

"Get up, Jo. Get your act together."

"Oh, hark at you," she flounced.

"It's your wedding. Everybody's wondering what you're doing."

"Shall I tell them what *we* were doing?"

He grabbed her arm and yanked her off the bed. "Look at you—you're a mess."

"That's the trouble with men. Once they've had their way with you—"

"Get dressed."

Coldly, he tugged at the disarranged wedding gown and pulled it to the floor. She laughed, stepping out of the gown and leaning against him for support. Her bra hung loose around her neck and when she flung it away she was entirely naked.

"Please Daddy, don't smack your little girl."

His anger was obvious. "This is your wedding party—but no one has seen you for damn near two hours."

Clumsily, she tried to put her arms around his neck. "Come on, Florian—"

He shook her off. "Get down there and see your husband."

★ ★ ★ ★ ★

Miro had just stepped onto the stairs when for the second time he met Florian coming down. Before Miro could ask what he was doing there, Florian called, "Miro! I was looking for you."

"Up there?"

"You had disappeared, sir."

They were together now, halfway up the stairs, the noise from the party forcing them to stand close to be heard. Miro said, "Jo's mother—she's had too much champagne."

"You want me to *spirit* her away?"

"If we call a taxi she might refuse to get inside."

Florian pulled a wry face. "She might refuse to come with me. I'm not her best friend."

There were people in the hall. Anyone might be listening. Miro whispered, "Have you seen Joanna?"

"Isn't she downstairs?"

Miro continued upwards. Florian would have preferred Miro not to find Jo in her present mood, but he couldn't prevent it. He continued down into the noise of the wedding party.

On the upstairs landing the party noise was dimmed. No one was up here. Miro glanced in the bathroom but she wasn't there. When he reached their bedroom he didn't knock but walked straight inside the room. Jo was sitting naked at the dressing table, studying herself in the mirror.

"My God," he said. "Anyone could have come in."

"But they didn't."

"I met Florian on the stairs."

He looked around the unlit room. The bed was a mess. Her wedding gown lay in a heap. On the bed was Dee's dress, a pillow, some underclothes . . .

"What the hell's going on?"

Jo's reflection stared at him. Normally when she was naked she looked vulnerable and young. But she looked older now. It must be the light.

"Florian?" she mumbled.

"He was going down."

"Oh yes?"

She started fixing her black hair. The action of raising her arms lifted her achingly young breasts. Miro swallowed as she peered at herself in the mirror. To see more clearly she opened her dark eyes wide.

Miro said, "Did he come in here?"

She turned slowly. "What are you saying?"

"Did Florian see you like that?"

"Naked?"

"Yes. For Christ's sake, Jo!"

"D'you think I'd let him into my bedroom?"

"He . . . He could have barged straight in."

"He'd knock."

"*I* didn't."

"It's your bedroom."

He couldn't understand her. Normally she was so easy to talk to. "What's happened here? The place looks as if a bomb has hit it."

"I'll tidy it later."

"Is something wrong?"

Jo sighed. "I've been trying to sleep."

His voice softened. "I know. It's not been the greatest wedding day. Are you feeling all right? After the excitement and champagne—you've had nothing to eat."

"I was just starting to get dressed."

"We'll get some food inside you. Some coffee."

"I'm not drunk."

"I didn't say . . . I'll take you downstairs."

"I can manage." She produced a friendly smile. "You go down. I'll be there in a minute."

He peered at her through the dimness. "Well, when you do come, you come straight to me."

Although the noise level stayed high there was a strangeness about the party, a sense of incompleteness, an awareness that the leading actress had not appeared. People murmured sympathetically that the disturbance in the church must have upset her, but beneath their tolerant words lay disapproval. Not to appear at all, but to come straight home and closet herself upstairs. Were they supposed to turn the music down? Was she storming about the bedroom? What had Miro taken on?

It didn't help that the bride's mother had to be assisted from the drawing room, out through the jostle of the hall, into the waiting Lexus outside the door. Miro had barely reappeared when Jasper buttonholed him. "Florian's taking Mrs. Beattie home. We had to bundle her into the car."

"The excitement," Miro mumbled.

"The champagne, more like. Anyway, she was too silly to resist. Florian's main concern was that she might be sick inside your car."

"Was she that bad?"

Jasper rolled his dark eyes. "Keep her at a distance in future, if I were you."

"Florian will look after her."

"Yes, we can rely on Florian."

Though they were in the less crowded rear hall they were not so out of sight that Dee could not find them. Better at holding her drink than Mrs. Beattie, she showed only a flush of rouge in her cheeks and a sharp sparkle in her eye. She took Jasper's elbow.

"Hi, lover."

Jasper froze. She said, "You don't have to ignore me, you know."

He smiled stiffly. "I wouldn't dream."

"It's all right. Your wife's pinned against the fireplace by some drip from your office."

A new tune started in the next room, something heavier.

"This is not the best time," Jasper muttered.

"I saw you pack Mrs. Beattie into the car."

"Didn't everybody?"

"It's a party. Who cares?"

She rubbed herself lightly against him but Jasper pulled away. Miro intervened: "Is Mrs. B often like this?"

"I've never seen her drink *champagne* before."

"But you've seen her drunk?"

Dee ignored Jasper and spoke to Miro. "I've hardly ever seen her since I left school. She and Jo aren't exactly close."

Jasper snorted. "Thank God for that." He glided away, twitching his head as if rocking to the music. "You say Lynette's in the drawing room—by the fireplace?"

"Oh, go find her yourself," Dee said curtly.

He glanced at Miro. "Well, if you don't mind?"

"While you're there, Jasper, light the fire. It's getting chilly with the doors open."

"Light it?" queried Jasper, looking pale.

"It's a gas fire, man. You only have to light the poker."

Jasper disappeared, looking as if he'd been sent on an important errand.

Dee spoke up above the louder music. "You've hurt his feelings now."

"I only asked him to light the fire."

"But Jasper isn't domesticated, is he?"

Miro's thoughts were elsewhere. "He can't be that incapable."

She regained his attention with a prod. "Not incapable, no—but I've known better." She grinned saucily. "I bet *you* know how to light a fire?"

He didn't take her meaning. "Yes, a house this size, no servants—you have to look after yourself."

"You've got Florian," she said.

He ignored her words again. "That man at the wedding this afternoon."

"Thomas?"

"You know him?"

"Of course." She had to step forward to make room for people passing behind her in the narrow hall. Someone said, "Hello, Miro." He smiled back. It was the wrong place for a quiet chat, and when the people had passed, Dee had to stay where she was, close against him. She said, "Thomas is Alan Pirie's brother. You know about Alan?"

Miro glanced nervously at people laughing nearby, but no one seemed to be listening. "Perhaps I don't know as much as I should."

She leant forward and squeezed his biceps. "It was years ago. Don't worry."

"What was years ago?"

She shrugged. "I wasn't with you in the vestry. What did he say?"

Miro didn't want to talk about it but he had to. To avoid shouting over the music he leant closer. "He said his brother and Jo were engaged."

"We all heard that in church. What else did he say?"

"That they're still engaged."

Dee glanced at their neighbours too, then leant closer still to whisper in his ear. "That's rubbish. Alan's just out of jail."

He turned his head in surprise. Their cheeks brushed. She whispered, "He was locked away for two years."

177

Miro withdrew several inches. "Jail?"

Dee gave a wry grin. "You older men."

"What does that mean?"

She was trying to be cocky but had a hint of sadness in her tone. "Maybe Jasper has the right attitude—take a young girl to bed, but never marry her."

Miro felt his cheeks sag. Music and laughter from the party merged into an ugly roar. It pounded in his ears and he felt old.

Dee was chattering again. "He won't be bedding *me* tonight, and that's for sure."

Miro tried to make small talk. "You can't have expected he would? He had to bring his wife."

"The best man always sleeps with the bridesmaid. Isn't that the idea?"

"Not at the best parties."

"Especially at the best parties."

"Well, Jasper is missing a great opportunity, I'm sure."

She touched his arm. "He's too old for me anyway."

"Thanks. Do rub it in."

Her hand didn't leave his arm. "Isn't Jasper older than you?"

"Rubbish."

Dee turned. "Oh, look who's arrived on cue."

She smiled at the stairs, and Miro had to step away from the wall to follow her gaze. He saw Jo coming slowly down in her burgundy dress. Her black hair was up, her skin was flawless and her slight smile looked painted on. Miro ran forward and took his young wife's hand. It was as if the guests had been waiting for her, because as she reached the bottom step the music stopped and several people began to clap.

She had only been downstairs an hour, yet to Miro it

seemed that the evening dragged on and on. He was more sober by the minute, while his guests seemed silly with drink; their skin looked blotched and puffy, their make-up cracked and smeared. It was as if he were the only sober one in the house, the latecomer to the party—yet Joanna was the latecomer, and she seemed light and happy. Whatever cloud had bothered her earlier must have passed. Now it hovered close to Miro. He tried to ignore it.

He asked her to dance with him again. Miro was a good dancer. The numerous parties he had to attend in his business life kept him up to date with the latest dance styles and he learnt each one studiously. Though there was something joyless in his dancing, no one could say that he looked old. He took Jo out onto the small dance floor and began an energetic routine. She bobbed effortlessly before him, using far less energy than he did.

"You look wonderful."

She smiled briefly, as she would at any compliment. "Funny things, weddings," Jo said.

"Why?"

"We get married, then we have this big party afterwards—when any sensible person would want to slip away and be alone."

Miro smiled happily. "We'll be alone soon."

"We should have gone straight off on our honeymoon."

"We will, tomorrow."

She smiled back. "That's not straight away."

Miro thumped his foot down on the beat. "It's like a lot of things in life—there are formalities we have to go through."

"But why should we obey the rules?"

He smiled encouragingly. "A pleasure delayed is . . . whatever, I forget now."

"Is a pleasure delayed. Why should we wait?"

179

He concentrated on his dancing. "You're sure you're all right?"

"I'm putting on a brave face."

Suddenly she stopped dancing and broke away. But she turned and stretched her hand to him. "Let's go out in the garden."

They went hand in hand, through the French window, people moving aside to let them through. The happy couple. Outside in the twilight the air had grown cool. One or two people wandered outside, but most stayed inside out of the chill. Jo and Miro stepped onto the lawn and crossed, alone now, to the still bubbling Three Graces fountain.

"I'm not getting in that again tonight!" chuckled Miro.

For a moment she didn't reply. Then she said, "You've said nothing about this afternoon."

"It's over now."

"It was all completely untrue, you know. I was never—"

"I know." He took her hand by the fountain. "You told me."

"But I *would* say that, wouldn't I? You must wonder, deep inside."

"I don't. You were never engaged to him, and that's that. God, the man hasn't been around for two years anyway."

"How do you know?"

"Dee told me," he said, his words slowing awkwardly as he spoke. "She told me about him being in prison."

"Dee," she said softly. "Always talking. Were you checking up on me?"

"No. She just told me."

"She certainly is some friend." Jo placed her fingers in the water at the rim of the fountain, shivered, but left her hand where it was. "It was Dee put Alan on to me, and gave him my address." She looked across the empty lawn towards the house, to music and waves of laughter. Everyone else was enjoying the party. "We should have gone away straight after church."

"It's easier this way."

"Is it?" She shook some water from her hand and stared at her fingers.

"Mhm. We can get a good night's sleep and start out fresh in the morning."

"Just like that."

He stepped closer. "What's the matter, darling?"

"Oh, I'm . . ." She splashed water again. "I really can't face this party. Everyone was there this afternoon. Every time they look at me they'll wonder."

He touched her wet hand. It felt cold. "Everyone's very fond of you—*I'm* fond of you. I love you."

She paused. "I'm sorry—I know I'm not what you wanted."

"You're exactly what I wanted."

She looked away. "Maybe things will be better in the morning."

"I'm sure they will."

"Look, when we go indoors I'll slip up to bed. No one will—"

"You can't go back to bed."

"Why not?"

"What will people say?"

"You see? We live by other people's rules."

"Darling, you can't go up to bed. It's your wedding day. You can't hide."

"That's true enough."

He took hold of both of her arms. "Jo, what's wrong with you? Do you . . . regret that we got married?"

She couldn't face him, but as he held her arms she knew

181

she should be looking in his eyes. She giggled childishly. "Oh, it's me, I'm being silly."

He relaxed, and kissed her fondly on the forehead. "It's been a trying day, darling, but it's nearly over. Let's go in together and try to hurry them along."

"That won't work."

"They'll get the message. It's getting late."

"Do I have to?"

He squeezed her arms. "I know it's a pain but this is something we have to do."

"Our duty?"

"Not exactly."

"Yes, it is—it's my duty, as a wife. Still, that's why you married me, isn't it—to be an . . . accessory."

"What does that mean?"

"That I'm . . . I don't know, a kind of trophy. Something extra. Here's old Miro, with a young wife on the side."

"Jo!"

"And now I have to go in and fulfil my new role."

"This is ridiculous. I don't know what's got into you—"

"Oh, something got into me, all right." She giggled nervously and squirmed out of his hold. "First night nerves."

"Is that all?"

"I can't do it," she said, backing away. "I simply can't do it."

He reached out for her but she skipped backwards. He said, "Come on, Jo. Let me help you—"

"No."

She backed further. He came forward, and suddenly she turned and ran. He began after her, but she was running for the open gate into the lane outside, and as Miro ran after her he realised that his young wife was simply too fast for him. He saw her disappear across the darkening lawns, then out through the wrought iron gate, and as the young girl ran so nimbly Miro cursed and felt his age.

Dee might be tipsy but she had noticed the peculiar atmosphere between Jo and Miro. She had followed them outside, and although she remained discreetly on the front steps, she had seen Jo run out through the gate. She waited while Miro hesitated on the lawn, then strolled down to meet him as he trudged back to the house. "It's only nerves," she said.

"I'm not nervous."

She took him by the arm. "Things have got on top of her, that's all."

Miro let her walk him along the path, away from the door. He said, "Well, that business in the church . . ."

"It was very upsetting—but it's over now—isn't it?"

He snorted. "Yes, everything's over, as far as I can see."

She chuckled and squeezed his arm. "Oh Miro, you're so dramatic! She's only gone for a cry in the lane. It's what women do."

"Really?"

"I thought you'd been married before? You're supposed to be experienced."

"I should have learnt, you mean?"

They had reached the stone steps leading down to the sunken side garden. Miro would have turned away but Dee continued on, pulling him gently after her. It was darker there, among the ferns.

Dee said, "When she comes back, I'll have a word with her. I'll tell her you understand. I'll say you're sorry."

"Sorry for what? I didn't do anything."

"Men! You don't know anything."

In the rapidly cooling lane Jo was conscious of her unsuitable shoes and burgundy dress. If she walked much farther she'd be in the village, and she couldn't possibly be seen there. She'd have to go back and face everybody and make it up with Miro. When she heard a car approaching she moved into the edge of the lane and walked on with her head bowed, hoping she'd be inconspicuous as the car went by.

But it slowed, then stopped behind.

His voice: "What's happened? Why are you out here?"

She heard him get out of the car, and she turned to face him in the lane. He had left the engine running. Jo shrugged helplessly. "I don't know what to do."

"Because of me?"

"Everything."

He watched a moment, then left the car and walked towards her. She waited. When he put his hands on her shoulders, Jo shivered. "Look at me," he said.

She raised her face. The hum of the engine lay in the lane. Florian lowered his head. She kissed his scar. When he kissed her properly, she opened her lips to meet his tongue with her own. They clasped each other, their bodies pressed so tight that he could feel her breasts against his chest and she could feel the rising hardness in his groin. He ran his fingers through her hair, tugging at the silky black tresses, pulling out the pins to let her hair drop down beside her cheek. She was open to him, her sweet face against his red ruffled cheek. Their bellies touched.

When they stopped, Florian leant back from her. He smiled in triumph but even he was amazed to see a similar light blaze from her eyes. They stared at each other ravenously.

"Where's Tommy?" she asked.

Hardly anyone was in the garden as the Lexus came

through the gate. Anyone who looked would have seen Florian in the driving seat. No one else. Jo was crouched on the floor behind his seat, chuckling with excitement as Florian delivered a laconic commentary.

"Twilight falls on Electra Court. A girl in a blue dress sits alone at the sparkling fountain—I don't know her name, but I want to call out *Bonsoir Tristesse*. Artificial light streams from the windows of the old house. In the fading light, the Lexus glides between parked cars along the drive. It is turning a corner now, moving along the front of the house, then round again. There is nobody here. Everyone's inside. Finally the car turns into the old cobbled courtyard that lies behind the main house. It stops. Wait—the driver is looking from side to side. But nobody is out here at the back. Nobody's watching. Now the driver will get out and open the rear door of the car. Then he'll walk no more than four paces to unlock the glass door on the right. When he's done that, the pretty girl in the back will slip softly from the car. She will run quickly across the cobblestones, into the sanctuary of the annex."

Chapter 17

To Jo the darkened annex was a foreign land. She had seldom been further than the simulated orangery that formed its entrance. In that antiseptic conservatory, shining plants waited for visitors who never came, cane chairs stood gathering dust, and the bizarre statue of a cherub posed alone. Tonight the green plants looked black in the darkness and the leaves hung in the air like fronds of jungle foliage in an old Tarzan film. Jo paused at the interior door to look behind her, through the glossy foliage and beyond the glass wall, across the courtyard to the rear of the house where her own wedding party continued noisily without her. People were in her kitchen. In the brightly lit window she could see them working: the catering staff, strangers in her house. A man was washing glasses, a woman setting a tray. Two young waitresses lounged against one of Miro's kitchen cabinets, pausing from their long evening of running backwards and forwards, serving guests. They were out of sight of the guests and didn't realise that anyone was watching them.

Florian said, "Quickly now. We've work to do."

He held the door to the interior corridor, also in darkness. All she could see of him was a shadowy outline. She said, "I like it here."

They had to feel their way along the inner corridor, because Florian said that any lights might still be seen. Only when he had found the door to the auditorium, when he'd un-locked it, when he'd pushed it open and they had slipped in-side, only when he'd closed the door with a clunk behind them, was Florian prepared to switch on a light. And in that final moment of absolute darkness, with the door closed and Florian fumbling for the switch, Jo heard a sound like a beast shuffling across the floor. There was a clink of chain, a muf-fled grunting noise. She felt for the wall—and the lights came on.

All three of them flinched in the sudden brightness. She and Florian averted their heads, but Thomas, who had been in total darkness for several hours, cowered as if he had been struck. He was gagged and chained to the base of a vertical steel girder, part of the working skeleton to the post-modern building. The room was multi-functional—primarily an audi-torium but with unanchored office chairs that let the small hall be used as a meeting room or training centre. At one end was a podium and a hanging screen, at the other end an en-closed projection booth. Two vertical girders stood each side of the hall, and the stanchions were joined by steel beams at the ceiling. The room was like an infilled steel cage. It had a hard vinyl floor.

Jo realised that the feral smell in the room came from the dark stain on the floor beside Thomas, who had urinated through his trousers. She felt disgusted. Surely he could have waited. He had only been there half a day. But his trousers were stained and there were marks on his knees, where per-haps he had slumped in a kneeling position into his own puddle of pee. He was trying to shout at them through the tightly fixed gag but he sounded like a man struggling to vomit. She could see him straining—it was ridiculous: his face had turned quite red. Perhaps he couldn't breathe. Thomas stamped his foot and Jo shook her head, surprised at him: that kind of behaviour would explain the bruises on his face.

Florian walked towards him but he stopped half way and turned back to Jo. "Your prisoner, ma'am," he said with a grin.

"Still alive," she murmured.

"And kicking, given half a chance."

"What'll you do with him?"

"I await your orders."

"Be serious."

Thomas growled through his dirty gag. He was a big man, heavier than his dead brother, and he pulled at his chain like a bear tethered at a stake. He glared at Jo. She found no difficulty in staring back at him, because tied and gagged, with his clothes so soiled, he resembled no one that she'd ever known. This wasn't Tommy. It wasn't a man.

She turned to Florian. "We daren't let him go."

"It *is* a poser."

He smiled briskly and walked across to the lecture podium. It was barely a foot above the ground but when Florian stepped onto it, he looked like an actor on a Jacobean stage.

He said, "You tell *me* what to do with him."

Jo looked at Thomas. "If we did let you go," she asked, "would you forget this ever happened?"

He shook his angry head.

She tried again. "Will you leave me in peace?"

His eyes said, "No."

Florian laughed from the stage. "What's a girl to do?"

"I know what I'd *like* to do," she said.

Florian smiled at her impishly. "What's that, I wonder?"

They stared at each other but she couldn't voice her thoughts. Florian said, "We'll have to ask Tommy."

She gave an irritated gesture and flopped down on a chair.

It swivelled. As Florian stepped from the stage Jo cocked a leg across the chair arm. If Florian had looked like an actor up there, she now felt like a stage director, watching from the auditorium. Florian went to Tommy and reached for the gag— but before he could touch it, Tommy lashed out with his foot. Florian skipped aside. Tommy was off balance now, and Florian danced straight back in with two blows to the ribs. They were not light blows, and Tommy could not protect himself. He slumped against the stanchion. Florian hit him once more, higher, this time knocking Tommy's head against the steel. Tommy's knees buckled, but he would not go down. He had been on his knees before, but he wouldn't kneel while they were watching him.

Florian ripped off the gag.

"You're free to speak," he said. "But shout all you will, no one can hear you."

Jo added, "The room's soundproofed."

Tommy made himself stand erect. Florian stood off, out of range of Tommy's feet, and said, "Everyone heard your speech today—despite which, Joanna is now married. So the dreadful deed is done, Tommy."

"Where's me brother?"

"He can't help you, Tommy."

Tommy's eyes narrowed. Florian added disarmingly, "I mean, he isn't here to help you."

"You killed him, didn't you?"

Florian gave a cold smile. "A deadly accusation."

Tommy stared at him. "I'm his brother. A brother knows his brother's murderer."

"That's an old wives' tale, I think. You have evidence?"

"I know what I know."

Florian strutted in front of the bruised and piss-stained prisoner but ignored him, speaking only to Joanna. "He'll go

on casting slurs. He seems determined to accuse one of us—
or perhaps both of us, Jo, think of that!—of murdering his
brother. Ridiculous, of course, though who knows? Perhaps
someone really did kill him."

Florian paused theatrically. Jo asked dully, "What happens now?"

"Things would be different if his brother's body ever did
float to the surface—"

Tommy grunted questioningly. Florian smiled.

"Figure of speech, Tommy. Now, Jo, think how people
will look at this. You were Alan's fiancée, and you didn't want
Alan to stop your marriage. You didn't want Miro to learn
that Alan had raped you—"

Tommy snorted angrily. "Raped her? Don't give me that.
She was beggin' for it. But he made her pregnant, didn't he?
Ask her what happened to the little baby."

Florian turned to her slowly. "A baby? Is that what you
didn't want Miro to hear?" She looked down. "Don't worry,
my love, he won't hear the news from me." He glanced briefly
at Tommy, then sat in a chair beside the silent girl and put his
arm around her. "What a fool this man is, worse than his poor
dead brother. It's quite plain he has to die."

He looked across at Tommy, who said, "You did kill Alan,
then?"

It was Miro's third whisky inside an hour, and with the
time approaching ten o'clock it was clear to Dee that he was
laying down a bellyful. The music was twenty years out of
date, but to Miro's guests those two decades made it easier to
dance to. They could throw themselves into the dancing,
looser than before, happy to toss back a drink, remove their
jackets and enjoy the fun. The more their faces creased with
laughter and drink, the more Miro seemed morose. He stood

by the fire, his back to the wall, watching merrymakers as if he were a watcher at the Masque of Death. His face had begun to develop a set belligerent look that should warn casual acquaintances to keep away. He needed a best friend, but Jasper was cavorting with his wife and, as Dee saw it, she and Miro were on their own.

"Come and dance with me."

"I'm happy here." He smiled grimly and raised his glass.

She took it from him. "You mustn't let people see you looking miserable."

She placed the glass on the mantelpiece and led Miro onto the floor. It was such an easy tune that he fell into it without thinking, and when he wasn't thinking he danced more easily. Anyone watching might have thought he was enjoying himself.

"Perhaps no one told you—this is a wedding, not a funeral."

"That's the one we celebrate, isn't it?"

"I prefer a funeral," Dee said. "When the worst is behind you, and you've something to look forward to."

He bobbed closer to her. "You know, don't you?"

She stayed in close. "It's been too much for her, that's all."

"She ran away."

"I know—"

"And didn't come back—"

"Isn't she in her room?"

"*Our* room, actually—not that you'd notice. No, she's not."

Neither of them made any pretence of dancing to the music. They let the rhythm move their feet but stayed head to head so they could talk.

"Where could she go?" he asked. "She doesn't know anyone in the village."

"Hitched a lift?"

"At this hour?"

Dee paused, her cheek against his, before asking innocently, "You're sure she didn't come back without you knowing?"

"I can't find her."

"There's nowhere *else* she might be?"

"We only have four bedrooms."

She grunted noncommittally, then said softly, "Oh, I'm sure that she'll come back."

Florian rammed the gag in Tommy's mouth. "He's had his chance to talk."

"Two's company," agreed Jo. "Three's a crowd."

She hadn't stirred from the low swivel chair, and Florian left Thomas at the wall and flopped into another seat beside her. They could have been theatregoers ignoring an usherette.

"He's lying. I was never engaged to Alan."

Florian put his arm round her. "But you bore his child."

"I didn't *bear* it."

"You ripped it out and threw it away."

"That's horrible! Anyway, you killed Alan. You cut his finger off."

Tommy growled but they didn't listen.

Florian said, "People will start looking for him eventually."

She chuckled. "His parole officer will, anyway."

"What do you want me to do with Tommy?"

"Stop him talking," she said lightly.

But he wasn't having that. "Say what you mean, Jo."

"What *do* I mean?"

192

Florian turned to Tommy, without moving from his chair. "These women, hey? Such termagants! It's obvious what she wants—but she won't say it."

Tommy glared at him, but Florian had been bouncing words off him. He smiled lazily at Jo. "You're so mealy mouthed. What d'you want me to do—just say the word."

"Advise me—"

"*You* tell me."

"I can't."

"But you're my mistress!" Florian turned again and laughed at Tommy—then seemed puzzled that Tommy did not laugh back. "Tell me, Jo."

He waited, until in a quiet voice she said, "You'll have to kill him, I suppose."

"But I killed his brother. It's your turn now."

"I couldn't. Stop playing with me."

"We're playing with Tommy."

He turned again to smile but Tommy gave nothing in return. He stared at Florian until Florian said, "Look at him—his eyes are bleeding from his brother's wounds."

"Be serious. How can we kill him and make it look an accident?"

Florian snorted. "A very accident prone pair of brothers. I don't think that will work."

"But if he's found dead . . . and everyone saw him at the church today . . . they're bound to suspect."

"Who?"

"Me, of course." She looked at him. "Or Miro—No, you can't do that to Miro."

Florian stood up. "Of course not. We need Miro." He took a step towards Tommy but he didn't step too close. "You really are a problem, you know? Perhaps we should kill you and hide your body. Would that be best?"

"You could put it where you put Alan's," Jo said.

"That's one solution." He was studying Tommy's large frame as if it were an article for sale. He nodded. "Women always like things neatly wrapped."

Dee walked along the upstairs corridor and paused at Miro's bedroom door. She cocked her head, listened, then without knocking walked in the room. No one was there. If she was disappointed she didn't show it. She glanced curiously at the unmade bed and the pile of bridal clothes, then walked across to the *en suite*. No one again.

Returning to the bed she lifted the crumpled duvet and peered beneath. She placed her hand on Jo's sheet. It told her nothing. She picked up Jo's wedding dress and began to carry it across the room to hang it up, but half way she stopped: why should she tidy their room? She should leave it as it was—let Miro read what he liked into its desperate disarray. As she dropped it back on the bed she noticed how grubby the dress was now—a black smudge on the side and a small creamy stain on the front. A piece of food or . . .

Dee glanced to the door, then with a slight hesitation raised the dress to her face and sniffed at the stain. It was difficult to be certain. To make out the smell for sure she'd have to practically rub her nose in it, and if the stain was what she thought it was she had no intention of doing that. When she dropped the dress again she made sure the stain was visible on top.

To Joanna it was like a dream. Things were happening around her over which she had no control. She had been stuck in the chair so long that her leg, cocked over the arm, had grown numb. She tried once to move it, and for a second or two it refused to move at all, then when it did move she felt a stab of pins and needles. She *could* move it, of course, but what was the point? She wasn't going anywhere, and there wasn't anything she could do. Florian had asked what she wanted him to do but he was playing with her. He had control. She stayed in the chair, leg cocked, head down, one arm trailing towards the floor. Her black hair obscured part of her face. In her formal burgundy dress she looked like a shop assistant on a break.

Florian said, "Let's not prolong the agony."

She looked up dully. In his raised hand he held a shotgun. He looked pleased with himself, like a magician who had produced a surprise out of thin air. But the gun did not impress her. Presumably he'd had it hidden in the room—perhaps behind the podium, or in the projection booth: who cares? He was like a magician, in his formal chauffeur clothes, his neat tie, his—yes, she realised what was so peculiar: he had put on a pair of gloves. Magicians often wore white gloves. He stood balanced lightly on his toes, inspired by the powerful shining weapon, looking to Jo for approval. She looked away, and for somewhere to look she glanced at Thomas chained to the wall. He was watching them, and his face, though distorted by the gag, seemed expressionless. He didn't try to speak—and it wasn't the gag that stopped him: he seemed as disinterested as she was. Florian was sparkling with electricity, while Thomas and Joanna seemed unplugged.

"Ready?" Florian asked.

"You can't do it here. They'd hear the noise."

"Can you hear their music?"

She paused a moment. "No."

"We're soundproofed." He laughed. "We're bomb proof, Tommy. What d'you say?"

Tommy stared at him. His eyes were dead.

Florian smiled at Jo. "Your turn to do the deed."

"No."

He handed her the gun but she wouldn't take it. She didn't flinch from it, she simply ignored it and kept her hands away. He said, "You know how to work it, I'm sure. Just point and pull the trigger."

"You trust me?"

"Of course." But he held on to the gun.

"Who do I point it at?"

He stared at her. "You and I are on the same side."

"You're wearing gloves. D'you want my fingerprints on the gun?"

He stared at Jo with hunter's eyes. "I said I trusted you, Joanna. Take the gun."

They both knew she wouldn't. After a moment he withdrew it and stepped back from her. Jo said, "That's Miro's gun."

"I don't own one, that's for sure."

"His fingerprints—"

"What's this obsession you have with fingerprints? We'll clean the gun."

"Afterwards."

"Yes, afterwards."

"When Miro's bullet is in Tommy's body. Very neat."

"This is a shotgun. They don't do ballistics with shotguns." He was angry now. "Why am I bothering to help you? You want to sort out your mess, you do it."

He held out the shotgun, but Jo knew that if she reached out and tried to take it he'd pull away. She watched the anger in his face.

"It's your mess," she said. "You shouldn't have told Tommy you killed his brother."

She felt great. Florian had been so dominant, but now she

had him on the ropes. She pushed herself from the chair. "You shoot him," she said.

He sprung forward and grabbed her hair. She laughed. "Go on, Florian—hit me. Shoot me—I don't care!"

He rammed the barrel beneath her chin. "I'll take your head off."

"Explain that away."

"I'll say Miro did it—"

Her laughter was like a scream. "It wasn't me, officer, it wasn't me!"

He used the gun to poke her head back further but with both hands she grabbed the barrel and twisted it aside. She was still laughing. She didn't care. "Not me. I couldn't cock my gun, officer. I couldn't get it up."

He raised the gun like a club but it didn't stop her. She screamed, "Go on, then, if you call yourself a man."

Suddenly he left her and marched across to the chained and gagged prisoner, and rammed the shotgun against his chest. Tommy raised his head as if to say something but he never made it. There was a massive bang and Tommy's upper torso seemed to collapse. He slumped forward and appeared to suck the gun barrel deep inside his fractured chest. His falling head barely missed Florian's face, and all the while Florian stared intently as if trying to catch the precise moment of his death. He removed the gun and let Tommy's body hang away from the stanchion like a broken figurehead on a boat.

Jo held her breath. Florian turned to her and bowed. "She who must be obeyed."

Dee walked slowly down the stairs, as elegant in her little red jacket as a film star on her entrance. One hand glided along the banister, her fingers barely touching the polished surface. She looked slowly from side to side, studying the guests in the hall as if they were extras in her film. Smoochy music hummed from the living room. The faces of the few guests in the hall looked tired—sagging from too much drink. She herself *had* been tipsy but she was sober now.

She reached the foot of the stairs and without a pause continued through to the large living room. This was where the life was. The hall had been a waiting room, an ante chamber to the feast. Some of the people out there were leaving, fetching coats. But in here the floor was crowded with slowly dancing couples, cradled in each other's arms, swaying vaguely to the music, drifting at that late hour into a fusion of drowsy bodies and an acceptance of what was to come.

Dee waited beside the dance floor till she saw him.

From Tommy's broken body thick blobs of congealing blood dripped like flakes of setting jam. His shirt front was a disgusting mess of red. When Florian lifted Tommy's arm the action was like that of a pump handle and for a few moments the blobs grew in size and flowed more freely. Though Florian tried to keep his hand clear a sudden red stain appeared on his white glove. He took the shotgun and tried to fit it into Tommy's limp right hand. He had to hold Tommy's hand inside his own, the gun in his other hand, and in trying to wrap Tommy's fingers around the trigger guard he seemed to be *wrestling* with the corpse. He seemed surprised that it was so difficult and Joanna, who had come a little closer—but not so close she might touch that expanding pool of blood—watched what he was doing with a puzzled frown. She saw Florian press Tommy's fingers around the unprimed trigger, then he stood back, removed his hand, and let the doctored shotgun fall to the floor.

She said, "They'll never believe it was suicide."

"I'll untie him."

"Why would he do it?"

"Broken heart?" he suggested, then he laughed and pointed at Tommy's mangled chest. "Looks like he died of one, anyway. Fancy a drink?"

He was staring at the blood stain on his glove and for a moment Jo thought he was suggesting they drink blood, but his mind had already flitted elsewhere: he started to wipe the white material on Tommy's shoulder, but it didn't cleanse the blood, it hardly shifted it at all. "Cold water," Florian said.

"I'll get some."

"What?" He looked at her with the vacant expression of a cat disturbed at its kill. "No, fetch the whisky. It's over there."

She glanced vaguely where he was pointing but didn't move. Florian stared at her intently but she knew he wasn't watching her; he was hardly aware of her at all. After a moment he slowly removed the soiled glove and placed that hand in his pocket to fetch out a key. He held the key between his teeth and pulled on the glove again. Then he reached behind the lifeless Tommy and unlocked a padlock on the chain. The body suddenly dropped forward and thumped to the floor.

Florian untangled the chain and stood with it dangling from his hand. "Two whiskies, please."

"Two?"

"We'll drink his health." Florian stepped away from the corpse. "Or *our* health. Somebody's." He nodded to the far wall.

"I don't think so."

He smiled at her. "Not feeling well?"

She took a breath, a deep one: it came surprisingly easily. "I'm feeling fine."

"That's my girl."

He smiled again at the thought, then walked across to the wall himself and picked up the bottle of whisky there. It was on a tray with four small glasses. He behaved as if the whisky were in no way incongruous, but merely poured two glasses and returned towards her with a glass held in each hand.

She said, "You're still wearing gloves."

"Of course. You'd better not touch that glass."

She hadn't intended to.

"Use your handkerchief," he said. "When you've finished your drink we'll put Tommy's prints on your glass."

She reached into the little side pocket of her burgundy jacket and took out a lace-edged hankie, so small it barely fitted round the glass. He watched her. He seemed as concerned as Jo that none of her prints went on the glass. When she was ready he said, "Cheers."

"Cheers."

"Good health. Long life."

They sipped their whisky. Florian didn't finish his. He approached the body and raised his glass to it. "Bottoms up. Down the hatch. Absent friends."

He drank his whisky and looked down at the corpse for a moment as if paying his respects. Then he marched to a small side table at the rear and deposited the empty glass.

"Finished?" he asked. "Please finish the drink."

There seemed no reason not to. When she knocked it back she was tempted to pour herself another, but she crossed to Florian. He met her halfway, reaching with his gloved hand for the glass. Before handing it to him she checked that her little hankie was in place.

"Wait," she said. "Better be safe than sorry."

She used one corner of the hankie to grip the rim and with the remaining scrap of material wiped round the glass. Florian chuckled. "You're quite right. Hand it here."

He polished the glass on his white glove. "Happy now?"

She nodded.

"You'll have to learn to trust me, Jo."

He walked across to Tommy and squatted beside him on the floor. Once again he took Tommy's lifeless fingers in his, and this time he fitted them around the empty glass. Jo watched as carefully as she'd watch a conjuror. But Florian did nothing clever: he simply fixed the set of prints, then stood up and took the glass to the little table at the rear.

"What happens now?" she asked.

"We go back to the party."

"I can't."

He smiled. "It's your wedding party. We must behave as if nothing unusual has happened."

"I'm not going back to Miro."

He studied her. "Not even for one night?"

"He won't expect me to. He saw me run away."

"Before I found you in the lane? Did anyone else see you?"

"I expect so. People were around."

"Unfortunate. If you don't come back it'll look suspicious. They might think you've run off with Thomas!" Florian laughed. "Until they find his body."

Miro knew he shouldn't dance with Dee again. It was his party—he could dance with anyone, especially with Joanna gone, but he had danced with Dee twice already. This was the third time, and she pressed more closely now. Her hands were round his neck and she settled into his shoulder. He had to hold her in his arms. He had to rest his hands flat against her back and feel her hard, firm body alive inside her tight red jacket. He had to press against her as she pressed against him, till both her soft breasts squashed against his chest and her perfume made his eyes water. He felt her thigh move between his legs and he knew she must feel the growing hardness of his erection. It wasn't fair. He shouldn't be aroused by Dee. He should be dancing with his wife. He shouldn't be cuddling a soft young blonde who seemed willing to take these cuddles further.

The music stopped.

That was the most telling moment, for they just stood there. Instead of politely thanking each other for the dance, they stayed on the floor among the other clutching couples, holding each other in silence till the next tune began. But it didn't begin. Miro looked up to see what was happening and saw the leader of the small band weaving through the stationary dancers across the floor towards him. The man had an apologetic smile on his face.

"Got to finish now," he said.

"What's the time? It's only . . ."

"Played half an hour over already."

The man shrugged self-effacingly. Pleasant as he was, he wouldn't shift. And somewhere in the back of Miro's mind was the feeling that it was probably just as well, that he didn't want to continue dancing, that if the music stopped and people went he could relax and stop pretending he was enjoying himself. Already he was cooling from the sultry heat he'd felt moments before. He could become businesslike again. Dee was still at his side—but she gave his hand a squeeze, said, "See you later," and disappeared. Sensible girl. Knew how to behave herself.

Not the sort to cause embarrassment.

Jo felt that the conference hall was growing larger. Either

that, or she was shrinking. The hidden lighting created pools of subtle light, but it also created shaded areas—not dark but less illuminated—until the rectangular hall seemed to lose its formal shape and become something harder to define. Without Florian it felt cooler. The one hot spot was by the side wall where Tommy's body lay on the floor. She wasn't frightened by it. He was so obviously dead. As soon as Florian had left the room she had tested for herself by going across to it and prodding the carcass with her shoe. It was like prodding against upholstery. After that she stayed away—there was too much blood where Tommy lay. She had gone to the small table at the rear to look at the two whisky glasses which Florian had so deliberately placed there. But she didn't move them. She wouldn't touch them ever again. She went round the hall to the other small table where the bottle of whisky stood on its silver tray. Two more glasses, as yet unused. She wouldn't touch them either. She looked at the whisky— Miro's malt, she realised. Miro's glasses. Miro's tray. Florian had worn gloves. He intended to frame her husband. But what had Miro ever done to him?

Come to that, what had Miro ever done to her, to deserve what she had done to him?

Poor Miro, she wished him no harm.

If she were sensible she could easily thwart Florian's plan. All she had to do was clean the glasses—or at least clean the three glasses that didn't have Tommy's prints. Not that anyone would believe the poor boy had shot himself. Why did Florian think they would? She decided to fetch a cloth, because she couldn't clean the glasses with her tiny handkerchief.

On her way to the door she looked back at Tommy's body and realised that his death didn't bother her at all. She reached for the door handle, then stopped.

Jo stood by the door for fully five seconds before putting her hand in the pocket of her burgundy jacket and drawing out the little lace-edged handkerchief. She used it to grip the door handle. Leave no prints. But what prints had she already left? She'd have to use the cloth to clean the arms of her chair.

The room was worse than cool now. The room was cold.

Florian had left her alone in the annex. He had left her with the corpse of a man who had blurted out her secrets in the church. He had left her at the scene of the crime, with a weapon, a motive and no believable excuse.

As the musicians packed up, the guests seemed anxious to follow their lead. Standing in his outer hall, Miro found himself shaking hands with a procession of guests in coats. He shook so many hands he felt like royalty. People wished him well and stumbled awkwardly through congratulations. Everyone knew that Jo had disappeared—though hopefully, they thought she'd run off to bed—but no one wanted to broach it with him. Men were bluff and women were too sweet.

Miro wore his mask-like face but he knew his tight-lipped smile was not reflected in his eyes. He felt detached from what was happening. He smiled in the faces of his guests, giving equal treatment to close friends and mere acquaintances, and he nodded at the musicians as they disappeared. He was aware that the catering staff had disappeared into the back. They'd be clearing up. Before long, all these strangers would have left his house.

He saw Florian making himself useful with the coats. Always neatly dressed, well spoken and polite, Florian was behaving like a butler. He didn't talk to Miro, just concentrated on the guests. They would remember Florian: a touch of class as they left.

Hardly anyone remained. Miro wandered into the vacated living room. Catering girls were collecting the last of the drinking glasses and party debris. Though the room looked a little bare there didn't appear to be any damage. The gas fire blazed in an attempt to bring homely cheer but this was a room from which all life had drained away.

Florian cracked a joke with the catering staff before slipping out the back door into the courtyard. A girl in the kitchen called Goodnight to him—a little wistfully, he thought. Her thoughts, like those of her colleagues, were on departure. Boxes were packed, their van was practically loaded, they would soon be on their way. Home to bed.

He paused on the cobbles to look at the sky. He had to look almost vertically up between the two buildings, and from the small patch that was visible the day's intermittent cloud had blown away. A few stars sparkled and a three-quarter moon shone down like a searchlight, casting a slanted light across the stone walls of the main house and converted stables. From the front of the house he could hear the last cars starting their engines. A door slammed. Someone called out.

When he stepped forward he caught a reflection of the distorted moon in the glass frontage to the annex. It was like a beacon from within. The glass was black, wet-looking, a mirror that reflected the distant moon but showed nothing behind. With each step he took towards it, the moon moved.

Miro watched her across the room. He wasn't surprised. He had given up being surprised. He didn't feel anything now.

He was leaning against the wall at the edge of the mantelpiece, the whole empty room before him, and when Dee appeared from the hallway she was like a character in a play. She walked deliberately towards him—but there was no one else in the room, so it was perfectly reasonable she should approach him. It was perfectly reasonable that she should still be there when all the guests had gone. She was the bridesmaid, after all. In her red jacket.

She continued towards him. He didn't move. At the last moment she swayed sideways and bent to warm her hands at the gas fire. He looked down at her. She crouched in profile, not looking at him, gazing instead into the clean yellow flames and crinkly porcelain logs.

She said, "I checked upstairs."

"Nothing?"

"Not even a forgotten coat." She moved closer. "I checked your bedroom."

"Checked or looked?"

"The bed's a mess."

Miro sniffed. "At least she didn't run off in her wedding gown."

"Something was spilt on it. Did you see?"

"She'd rubbed against the garage wall."

Dee changed the subject. "This is terrible for you, Miro." He didn't answer. "Spending your wedding night alone." He remained silent. "I mean, it's not so bad for me—I didn't really expect to sleep with Jasper. But what are *you* going to do?"

When Florian went through the conservatory to the corridor he didn't expect to hear a noise. But when he went into the lecture room he was surprised that Joanna wasn't there. He glanced left and right, the length of the hall. She wouldn't be behind the screen. He peered at the projection booth and though he knew she wouldn't be there he went to it anyway and peeped inside. He was going to ignore Tommy's body because he was dead, but there was something unavoidable about a body in an empty hall, so Florian strolled down to look at it. The blood had long since stopped flowing and it was easy now to pick a spot where there was no chance of accidentally getting blood on his shoe. And in the same way that he couldn't avoid going to stand by Tommy's body, he couldn't resist prodding it with his foot. It was just a body, no different to the touch than when alive.

He pushed with his foot and tried to tell whether he could feel it stiffening through his shoe. It was firm, although it gave a bit. With his toe resting on the body he glanced quickly towards the door. Then he raised his foot and brought the heel down sharply, kicking into the flesh hard enough that anyone living would jump in pain. But nothing happened. The corpse just lay there.

Florian shook his head in irritation. This was silly: he knew Tommy was dead—he couldn't be more dead. Half his chest had been blown away. He had taken the full charge of Miro's shotgun—

Where was the gun?

It was dangerous. Bloody dangerous. Anyone could walk in. Miro kept his back to the fireplace, and as he kissed her he kept his eyes trained on the doors. But there was silence in the house now. They were as alone just after midnight as any ordinary husband and wife. But it didn't feel like husband and wife. She was young and sweet like Jo, but unlike Jo she craved for sex. Dee squirmed against his chest, she gripped his back, her tongue glided into his mouth and the wet warmth of her lips felt like a fever. Jo had never kissed like this. Jo was beautiful and young but she was passive, compliant; she behaved like a dutiful wife. She *had* behaved like—

He gasped.

Dee was far from passive. The palm of her hand was on his zip. He could feel her fingers, could feel her nails. It was as if the cloth of his trousers was not there. He kissed more passionately and was so absorbed he closed his eyes.

When she finally broke the kiss Miro stood floundering like a baby plucked from a bath. And like a towel, Dee wrapped herself around him. She placed a hand at the side of his head. The other hand stayed where it was.

He realised that his own right hand had moved from her back and had slid around to find her breast. But while Dee's fingers were so alive, his own desperate fingers were hampered by the stiff cloth of her raspberry jacket. He ran his hand higher, to where the lapels parted at her collar bone, and when he brought his hand down Dee seemed to stoop slightly, and his hand slipped easily inside her wire-front bra, and with a rush of joy he cupped her breast. Her nipple was like a hidden button.

He scrabbled with his other hand to undo her jacket.

"Not here," she said.

"Everybody's gone."

"Upstairs," she said.

Florian checked his bedroom. She wasn't there. He was fully awake now, treading softly as he went. His eyes were sharp; they never stopped moving. While in the bedroom he checked the closet. He even looked beneath the bed.

Out in the corridor he opened the door to his tiny kitchenette. He switched on the light. Nowhere to hide. He glanced at the floor-level cupboards. Surely too small.

There was another meeting room. He looked inside. It was a small room; Miro called it a breakout room, whatever that meant. But it was as empty as it had been for several months.

She had run away.

He considered the options. Would she have run away again, along the lane? After midnight? Not a chance. Perhaps she had the car. He had the Lexus keys in his pocket but Jo might have another set. Seemed unlikely. And Miro would never have given her the keys to his Ferrari. So perhaps she had gone back to the house to get some car keys.

Wherever she was she wasn't here.

Florian moved back into the dark conservatory. Across the way the catering staff had switched off the kitchen lights, and the only light from outside was a spill of moonlight, dimly illuminating the cobbled courtyard, so he seemed to be looking out through smoked glass. Fronds and leaves of large formal houseplants hung in the translucent air. If the path to the conservatory door had not been wide and central he would have barely been able to pick it out between the plants. He was halfway along when he heard a sound.

The shotgun ratchet.

He peered to his right. Deep in the foliage stood Joanna, the shotgun pointing at his heart. She wasn't used to guns. She held the butt into her hip and pointed the barrel like the nozzle of a vacuum cleaner.

He whispered, "What are you doing there?" He couldn't see her face.

"You set me up."

"Excuse me?"

She shifted her stance, but the gun never wavered. She said, "Me and Tommy, the gun, the glass with my fingerprints."

"We cleaned them off."

Florian stepped off the path.

"Stay where you are."

He cocked his head. "You know how much noise that makes?"

"I was there, remember."

He stepped towards her.

"I'm serious, Florian."

He nodded. "What did you think I'd do—send someone across to see what they might find?" He waved a disarming hand, brushing through the leaves. He could see her features now. "I killed for you, Joanna. Twice, in fact. I took care of everything. But you still don't trust me."

"I was afraid," she whispered.

Florian's shoulders slumped. "I've given you everything, and you'd shoot me like a dog." He smiled through the darkness. "Without you my life is not worth living."

"Don't give me that."

"Will you shoot me if I come nearer?" She didn't answer. Florian shrugged. "Since I've nothing to live for, let's find out."

Slowly, one step at a time, he began towards her. On the second step she raised the gun. It was butted in her stomach now, even more precarious than before. He opened his arms and exposed his chest. "Shoot me."

He approached until the barrel jabbed against his chest. "Last chance, Joanna."

She couldn't pull the trigger. He waited till she lowered the gun, then as she was about to toss it aside he grabbed it, spun it into a shooting position and raised it calmly to his own head. "Come on, I'll do it."

"No!" she screamed.

"Ssh."

He placed his free hand across her mouth, and used the other to raise the gun barrel until it prodded his scarred cheek. "I've nothing to live for, Jo."

He pulled the trigger.

It clicked.

Florian lowered the gun. "It only had one cartridge."

Her knees buckled, but he lifted her. Pulled her close.

"Oh God," she sobbed. "I'm sorry."

She was dampening his chest. He raised her head. "Don't worry. *You* didn't pull the trigger."

"But I didn't trust you."

"And now you do." She nodded. "Like I trust you."

Miro stands with Dee in the bedroom doorway, looking at the wrecked bed and disordered room. "What was she doing?"

"Better you don't know."

He steps into the room and stares at it. Dee can see his mood shifting and she comes quickly to wrap her arms about him. She nuzzles his neck. He doesn't react. The one thing she does not want is a night in bed with a man who cannot get it up. Guilt or no guilt, husband or not, he has to do the business.

She stands in front of him. "Kiss me, Miro."

Hot lips. Warmth and wetness. Her hand stroking the small hairs on the back of his neck. Tingling perfume. Sighs of appreciation. He starts responding.

She takes his hand and rests it on the buttons to her little raspberry jacket. He undoes the buttons, his face glued to hers, and feels her through the brassiere, taking his time before sliding his hand round to unclip the fastenings. They spring free and her soft flesh makes him gasp. She pulls him closer, till she feels his resurgence through layers of unyielding cloth. Now she can bring her hand round. Let her fingers do the talking.

Miro's lips are feeding on her breasts, but he is awkwardly stooped, so she leads him to the unmade double bed. When they crash down on it she falls into a soft mound of duvet and bridal clothes. White lace froths round her head, and she doesn't know whether the soft material is from Jo's dress or her own. She is pulling at Miro's clothes. His tie is gone. His shirt is ripped off and flung away. She has both hands on his trousers, unclipping the belt, sliding the zip.

He is practically naked, and he slides down her body, nuzzling her yielding breasts again before continuing down to remove her tight black skirt. Off come her undies. Nothing left. Miro and Dee writhe across the rumpled bed, crawling over each other, running their hands into moist intimate crevices, pressing against each other, tumbling among the tangled linen and bridal lace. Dee is aroused by the soft material. She grabs handfuls of white organza and holds it to her skin, and Miro pushes them away as if the scraps of white are the last remnants of clothing with which Dee can protect her modesty. He has become the lustful invader, the rampaging hero, and she is the plucky heroine forced to submit to him on the bed.

And yet with one hand, one grabbing movement, heroic Dee guides Miro inside her and leans back, her head dangling off the mattress, her hands for a moment thrown back as if held by collaborators in a gang rape. She is fully open to him. He can have his way with her. He can do anything he likes. Her head is back and she cries out as if he is hurting her, but Miro knows what she is doing; he rises to the game and thrusts harder, deeper, stronger—driving the naked woman into the frothy bridal bed. They shout so freely that every stroke could be their climax, until suddenly there is no mistaking it—he yells like a wounded animal—they both call out, and from the sounds they make and from the way that Dee and Miro collapse and lie quivering, anyone might think that a murder had been done.

Florian was cross with her—not that she'd threatened

him with the gun, but that she'd caused them both to leave their fingerprints on it. He sat on an office chair in the lecture hall, the gun across his knees while he polished it with beeswax. He had his white gloves on again, the fingers marked with wax like nicotine stains, and he concentrated on rubbing every part of the empty shotgun. He had rubbed it down, rewaxed it, and was now polishing it again. With his hands inside those cotton gloves, and in shirt and tie, he reminded her once again of an exotic conjuror—a sorcerer, perhaps—performing a trick. She kept her eyes on him for sleight of hand.

While Florian rubbed at the gun, Jo paced the hall to the stage, back again, back to Florian—but never too close to Tommy's body on the floor. Though the corpse seemed less threatening now, part of the furniture.

Florian finished and stood up. Still wearing the gloves, he stepped across to Tommy and took his hand. He wrapped the dead fingers around the trigger, pressed them to impress a mark, then removed the hand and laid down the gun. He took Tommy's other hand and placed it halfway along the barrel, beneath the stock, to where it might it have been had Tommy ever held it. He pressed again, then removed the hand and laid the shotgun beside the body. The butt of the gun lay just inside the pool of blood. That artistic touch seemed to appeal to Florian.

Jo said, "We can't leave him here."

"Why not?"

"You're trying to frame Miro. That isn't fair."

He studied her, as if she were another piece of the tableau he had to arrange. "It's a safety precaution."

"How?"

"If someone finds the body before we move it, we won't be blamed."

"But why *can't* we just take it away?"

He shook his head. "It's the middle of the night. We'd make too much noise."

"Everyone's gone now."

"Miro hasn't."

She fell silent. In the soundproofed hall there was no noise. Florian smiled at her.

She stammered, "But if someone found it, we'd be here. They'd blame us."

"Who's going to come into the annex? No one does."

She stared at him. "Then why are you setting it up like this? The fingerprints. The gun."

"What does it look like?"

"Miro's gun. You're framing him. He doesn't deserve it, Florian."

"Miro's gun but Tommy's fingerprints. It was suicide."

"They'd never believe that. How'd he get the gun?"

"We'll say Miro stores it here."

"But he doesn't. He'll know we're lying."

"If Miro finds you here with me he'll *know* we're lying." Florian stepped towards her and put his gloved hand on her arm. "But he won't find you here."

Florian held both her arms, then pulled her gently to him. "We can't do anything till tomorrow, Jo. We don't need to. No one will give Tommy any thought, and I'll pop over to the house at breakfast and commiserate. You stay here. Maybe later tomorrow you should phone him—pretend you're in London or somewhere. Say you're at your mother's—he won't go there!" Florian laughed. "See? Everything's under control." He glanced contentedly round the room. "Now, Jo my love, since we're finished here, we might as well trot off to bed."

He began to lead her from the room, but she dragged behind. "We can't just go to bed as if nothing's happened. I couldn't sleep."

Florian laughed again. "Who said anything about sleep?"

Chapter 18

Jo hadn't realised there would be daylight. Till now, the long hours she had spent in the annex had been in darkness or artificial light. But today as the pale morning light seeped into Florian's tiny bedroom the walls took on a different tint. They looked cooler, cleaner. The sky outside appeared palest blue. His window looked out behind the annex, away from the main house, across an unused yard, a scrap of grass, and over the low rear stone wall to gently rolling fields behind. This was what Florian saw each morning.

She sat up in bed and he reached out and stroked her shoulder. When she looked down at him he held her gaze and ran his hand down onto her breast. She could see possession in his eyes, a quiet triumph that when he touched her now she did not flinch. Then he tilted his head to present her with the unblemished side of his face. He ran his thumb across her nipple and watched her intently. She gave no reaction, holding herself back, not prepared to let him see that he aroused her. He held the full weight of her breast and stroked oh, so softly. Beneath the sheet his other hand was on her leg and she realised that when he moved higher he'd find that, despite the coolness she showed, she was moist.

Why did she sit here like the ice princess? She was like a schoolgirl playing statues, letting the schoolboy—the risible, harmless schoolboy—stroke her, feel her, tickle her, but

216

never letting him see her move. She looked into Florian's eyes, deep brown stones shining through water, and in their depths she saw his confidence, his teasing arrogance, even a pale fleck of animal cruelty. She could easily move to see the other side of his face, but she didn't. Florian panted softly. She could feel his breath upon her arm. She was tense while he was relaxed. He was ready for her, she knew.

Why did she hold back? She moved to look at the whole of Florian's marred face. It didn't repel her now. He edged a little closer and she began to feel his heat. She saw his muscles move. He was so strong. His fingers played with her and she gasped, quivered, ceased to be a statue and gave in.

Jo flung herself across him. Her small white body pressed against him like a child clutched by its father, except that now for the first time she behaved nothing like a child. She slammed her open mouth on his, shot her eager hand to his groin and explored him as she'd never felt a man before. Then she took his heat deep inside herself and straddled him, impaled herself, gave herself up to a surging rush of power and a pleasure more intense than she had ever known. She pushed her hands down on his strong shoulders, supporting herself in this way while she bounced deliriously up and down. And Florian let her—he lay back as if Jo's tiny weight had pinioned him to the bed, as if her tiny hands on his big shoulders were enough to hold him down. And he laughed. His strong warm thighs pulsed beneath her in harmony with her own.

She opened her eyes. The blue sky had become less pale now. She felt the warm summer sun wash over her, but when she moved her arm she realised that it wasn't the sun—it was the heat of the bedclothes which Florian had pulled back over her as she slept. She reached out to thank him but he wasn't

217

there. In panic, she half sat up. But he hadn't left her—he was getting dressed, and he smiled across the room.

"I have to work."

She sat up fully, deliberately letting the bedclothes fall away to reveal her breasts, and she smiled wickedly. "You're not going to leave me with nothing to remember you by?"

He knotted his tie. "You getting up?"

She stretched, but he wasn't watching her. "I'm not going anywhere."

"Yes, you are."

To her astonishment, he had started pulling on a clean pair of white cotton gloves.

"What are you doing?"

"I have to put the gun back." He reached in his pocket, pulled out two cartridges and showed them to her. "Miro keeps the gun loaded, naughty man. By the way, I've been thinking: you'd better go across first—and apologise to him."

"Apologise!"

"His wife walks out on him straight after the wedding? He'll want more than an apology. Even a gold digger would sleep with her husband once."

"I'm not a gold digger."

"Why did you marry him?" He grinned down at her—a cold grin.

She clutched the bedclothes to keep out the chill. "I was fond of him—"

"Fond? Oh, you *were* fond, I see. What do you feel now?"

"Don't be mean with me. I *was* fond of him. He seemed so solid and reliable. After Alan, you know, he seemed so . . . *right*." She stared at Florian, hoping he might understand. "I shouldn't have married him, of course. It was . . . immaturity, I suppose. I don't know what it is with me, but every new man—there haven't been many, honestly, not many men at all—but every new man seems to erase the previous one. Each new one seems so perfect, and the old one . . . becomes so ordinary. I end up wondering what I saw in him."

She petered out, staring at the shape of her legs beneath the bedclothes. He asked, "What do you see in Miro now?"

"Oh, I still like him. I'm sorry I did this to him."

"Fine. Go across and tell him that."

Jo let herself in the front door—the back door might have shown she'd been at Florian's—and was hit by an immediate smell of stale alcohol and dead tobacco. More than the stink she felt the strangeness—this was not how Miro's house should smell. The bare front hall looked unfamiliar, as if a crowd had rushed through it, as if the house had been burgled. It looked cold and desolate, yet was far from cold. The heat of all those bodies seemed to have been trapped in the hall. She reopened the front door to let in some air.

When she went into the empty living room the sense of a ransacked house grew stronger. Furniture had been pushed aside for the party and the floor was littered. Even the walls seemed grimy. The room was hot and stuffy, like a station on the Underground before a train came roaring in. The gas fire had been left on all night. It blazed in the hearth as neatly as when first switched on, the porcelain logs pristine and newly laid. Jo shook her head. Before switching it off she went to the large front window and opened it full. She paused a moment to look across the rose beds and long lawn, then turned back to look at the room. She was crossing to the fire when she heard a sound in the hall. Someone on the stair. That would be Miro, coming down. She must be ready for him.

Jo took position at the mantelpiece and stood with head erect, waiting till Miro came in. She watched the door until it opened. They stared at each other—Jo motionless at the fireplace, Dee with her hand on the living room door.

"I thought you were a burglar."

She broke her stare to smile at Jo, a nervous smile.

"I like the dress," Jo said.

Dee was wearing Joanna's wedding gown. It looked loose on her. It was not done up.

"I'm sorry." Dee smiled again, leaning against the wooden door. "We're the same size, almost."

"One size fits all."

Dee came hesitantly forward. The way the unfastened dress hung, Dee should have tottered across the room, but she glided like a child. Jo saw she was barefoot. On her blonde friend the loose white wedding gown looked tawdry. Her hair was wild, her make-up smeared, her eyes ringed with soot.

"Where have you been?" Dee asked.

"I came back."

Dee nodded. "Did you stay at the flat?"

Jo looked at her, then nodded. Dee asked, "On your own? Or . . ."

"Meaning?"

"That was some party last night. I guess we both had too much to drink." Dee licked her lips. "It happens, you know? Some parties are just like that."

"Just another party."

Dee came closer. "Look, I'm sorry, right? I was stupid. We were all stupid."

"You slept with Miro?"

"Don't get on your high horse, Jo. You're not exactly the virgin bride yourself."

"What's that supposed to mean?"

"Where were *you* last night?"

"In my flat. You said it yourself—"

"How did you get back? I didn't hear the car arrive."

Jo shook it away. "You slept with my husband—on our wedding night!"

"Well, where were *you?*"

"That's an *excuse?*"

"You were fucking Florian, weren't you?"

"Florian?"

But it wasn't Jo's voice. There in the doorway stood Miro, in his dressing gown. His hair was tangled and he planted his bare feet on the floor. "Is that where you went last night?"

"Well, what were *you* doing?"

"You slept with *Florian?*"

"You slept with *her!*"

"Oh, excuse *me*," scoffed Dee. "I'm a shuttlecock."

Miro marched forward. "How long has this disgusting . . ." He couldn't finish.

Jo cut across: "Oh, it's disgusting when *I* do it, but it's all right for you and this—whore?"

"But Florian—my chauffeur? How could you do this, Jo? I don't believe it."

"Well, I did. And I loved it! He's worth a hundred of you."

Miro towered over her and for a moment she thought that he would hit her. They were head to head and she blazed at him, daring him to strike her, but in the first flicker of his gaze she knew he'd never hit her.

As he headed for the door she called, "Go back to bed! The only place you'll have me now is in your dreams."

He slammed the door behind him.

Dee asked, "How long have you been sleeping with Florian? I *knew* you were. You can't hide anything from me."

"It was your fault. If you hadn't slept with my husband, on our *wedding* night, he would never have known."

"Well, exactly, it was his wedding night—*someone* had to sleep with him."

"And you loved it, didn't you?"

"Come on, Jo, you can't be serious about *Florian*."

"Why not?"

"He's a driver. He's nothing compared to Miro."

"I don't want *Miro*."

"Jo!"

"You're welcome. You looked after him last night. Well, here's my thanks!"

Jo slapped her face, and when Dee staggered in surprise, Jo pushed her backwards towards the fire. Dee caught her foot against the fireguard. She stumbled and her head cracked against the mantelpiece. Jo continued to shout as Dee fell down. She was still shouting as flames nibbled at the wedding dress: "See what you've done, Dee, you stupid bitch? You've ruined it. You've ruined everything!"

She turned round and stormed after Miro. Where did he think he was going? What did he mean to do? She never looked back at her friend, her bridal dress, the flames racing over Dee's body in the hearth. Dee didn't matter any more. She was not worth thinking about. She had caused this, and would pay dearly for her weakness.

Jo rushed across the courtyard, through the open glass door into the annex, knowing the moment she saw the open door that Miro was ahead of her. She ran through the conservatory, plants swaying in the draught she caused, then along the rear corridor. Where were they? She heard their voices— Miro's voice. He roared: "Give me that!"

Florian muttered something. She couldn't hear.

Miro shouted, "Do as you're told!"

She burst into the lecture hall to find Miro a yard in front of the nonplussed Florian. Florian held the shotgun. Was he offering it or threatening Miro? She couldn't tell. As Florian turned his head towards her, Miro grabbed the gun and wrenched it away. Florian gave no resistance. She ran across the floor and stopped halfway.

Miro held the gun across his chest, raised but not pointing at Florian. For a moment, Florian seemed smaller than she remembered him. He stood poised on the balls of his feet, eyes glittering. He could snatch the shotgun; she was sure of it. Yet he stood waiting.

"How could you do this, you bastard?"

"We *had* hoped to hide it from you." Florian looked aside at Tommy's body on the floor. "But we hadn't time to get rid of the body."

"You slept with my wife!"

"We couldn't drive off with him at night. You would have heard."

"*Didn't* you?"

"We meant to hide the body this morning. You need never have known."

"I'm not talking about that!"

Florian leant forward, touching his arm, making no move for the gun. "But it's murder, sir. A serious crime. You don't want to be mixed up in that."

"Murder?" Miro dithered with the gun. It was as much use in his hands as a mop. "What on earth made you kill him?"

"He was annoying your wife, sir."

"*Annoying?* You killed him for that?"

"She couldn't take those accusations. You might have believed them. A jealous husband believes anything."

Jo stepped forward. Miro seemed momentarily speechless. Florian turned to her apologetically. "We'll have to tell him."

"Better not."

Florian reached a friendly hand towards Miro—but this time reached for the gun. Miro stepped smartly back, raising the shotgun and ramming the barrel to Florian's chest. Florian raised his hands good-humouredly. "Gosh, Miro. We'd better put that somewhere safe."

Miro snarled, "Stay where you are." He turned to Jo, keeping the gun on Florian. "See what you've done?"

"Put it down, Miro," she demanded.

Florian said, "Don't blame her, sir. She wasn't herself last night."

"That's an *excuse?*"

"Perhaps not in law, sir—but Thomas kept going on. Eventually she shot him."

"She—*Joanna* shot him?"

"Oh yes, sir."

Miro glanced towards her. Florian's hand flicked for the gun, but Miro jumped and stuck it again in his chest. Florian stepped back, hands raised and a half smile on his face. "Careful, sir. That could go off."

Jo said, "Please, Miro, put it down."

Miro said, "I *should* shoot you, Florian. Why not? When did this start?"

"Well, Tommy came to the church—"

"When did you first fuck my wife?"

"Excuse me?"

"You heard."

Florian looked bewildered. "Who on earth told you that?"

"*She* did!"

"Joanna?" Florian frowned at her. "Mrs. Vermont?" He reached his hand for her. "Did you say that?"

She began towards him.

Miro snapped, "Stay there."

But she ignored him and took hold of Florian's outstretched hand. Miro wavered between them. He said, "Don't try to deny it."

Florian grasped her hand firmly. "How could we? With Tommy's body there on the floor."

Miro followed his glance—and Florian pulled Jo between them. She brushed against the gun, knocking it briefly aside. As Miro swung the gun back, Florian held the girl like a shield, saying, "Dead body, sir. Your gun. Your prints on the gun."

Miro tried to force the gun around Jo but she was helping Florian now, keeping her body between them and grasping the shotgun herself. She laughed in Miro's ashen face. "You'll get the blame for it, Miro—not us!"

"I'll kill you."

"Kill everyone! You killed Tommy, you killed Alan—"

"*I* killed them?"

They were still struggling for the gun.

"Yes, Miro—that's what the police will say. So kill *me*. Blast me away."

"Stupid bitch!" snapped Florian. He reached round her and secured his own grip on the gun. "I had her, Miro." He heaved at the gun. "I earned her love—and I *enjoyed* my reward!"

Jo was trapped between the two men. She twisted and beat against Miro's chest.

Miro wouldn't release the shotgun.

"She's so sweet," Florian jeered. "So sweet I drunk her up. Every drop."

Jo was still in the way. She tried to snatch the gun. She pushed sideways, and as she crashed against the gun it blasted by her side. She tumbled to her knees and slithered on the floor, the explosion ringing in her ears. She looked up. Then screamed. Miro stood with the gun hanging from his hands. Florian was several feet away, flat on his back, his white shirt puddled with blood. He twitched on the floor. Joanna howled and crawled across to him. She ignored the growing stain of blood and knelt beside him. He looked up at her.

"Can you see me?" she asked.

He seemed to nod. But Florian's movements meant nothing now. She cradled his maimed face and said, "Don't leave me behind."

It was as if he suddenly fell asleep. He gave a kind of snore, a shudder, then on his slackening lips emerged a childlike bubble of frothy blood.

"It's over," Miro muttered.

Jo looked up at him from the floor. Miro still had the gun, but it was as lifeless in his hands as Florian. The barrels pointed at Miro's feet. Joanna turned back to Florian, smears of blood on her knees and hands. Softly, reverentially, she placed the back of one bloody hand against his withered cheek. Already, the life that had flowed so vigorously had gone. Flecks of blood lay on his lips. His open eyes had dulled.

She heard Miro ask her, "Why?"

"He was a man worth loving."

Jo got to her feet as creakily as an old lady. "You'd better give me the gun."

He shook his head faintly. "Are you going to shoot me too?" she asked.

He stared at her.

She stepped towards him and with the gentle authority of a mother took the shotgun from his hand. "I couldn't kill you," Miro said. "Despite everything."

"No," she said. "You couldn't. But *he* would."

She smiled ruefully as she raised the gun. The blast

226

knocked her backwards—but sent Miro several feet farther. He lifted in the air, seemed to hover, then crashed to the ground. Jo didn't even look at him. As the reverberations settled in the soundproof room a numbing calmness fluttered down on her. She felt anaesthetised. Calmly, Joanna reached in the pocket of her burgundy jacket and took out the little lace hankie from the night before. She put her hand in the other pocket and gripped the gun barrel through its cloth. Then she began polishing blood and prints from the trigger and its guard.

As she cleaned, she hummed tunelessly. "That's what Florian would do."

When Joanna went through the conservatory the plants seemed to shake into life. She walked out onto the cobbles, saw the open kitchen door but decided against going straight indoors. She needed some air. She needed to think. As she strolled to the side of the main house she caught an acrid smell, a bonfire maybe, early Autumn leaves. Quite a pleasant smell. It wasn't till she approached the front that she realised that the house was on fire. Dark smoke billowed from the front. But Jo walked at the same unbroken speed till she reached the corner and when she got there she saw smoke rolling out through the open front window. She studied the smoke as if it were a curiosity arranged for her inspection. When she stood by the rose bed she could see flames inside the living room. It was hard to see clearly through the smoke, but it was interesting, she thought, exciting. When she turned her cheek she felt the intense heat.

It seemed several days ago that she had knocked Dee into the fireplace. Could she still be there, lying in the wedding dress like a melting doll in Miro's hearth? She must be, Joanna thought. The flames must have run out across the floor. That fine wooden floor. Miro had been so proud of it. Original, he said. All that wood to burn.

She saw more smoke beginning to emerge from the room above. She gazed at the mullion window and nodded, as if it made a kind of sense that their bedroom was to be cleansed by fire. She thought it unlikely the flames would destroy everything. Eventually, when men picked through the wreckage, they'd find Dee in Jo's wedding dress, with a crack on the head. Jo winced at the thought. She stepped nearer the house. Perhaps there was still time to get in there and . . .

There wasn't. The heat was increasing. Deep in the smoke she saw sparks among the flames. It was an ugly fire, she decided, not homely at all, and the smell had become disgusting. She walked around the rose bed and onto the lawn, so she could traverse the front of the house, watching as the fire took greater hold, but keeping herself safe from the flames. What would happen now? The fire brigade would come—then the police. She couldn't stop them. Joanna sighed. They couldn't prove she had killed Dee—anyway, it was an accident, wasn't it? Everything was an accident. No one should pay. Miro had shot Florian, accidentally. Someone had shot Miro—accidentally also, in a way. It couldn't have been her—she had not been there. The only prints on the gun were Miro's. So he'd shot Florian, just as he'd shot Tommy, the police would say. Just as he'd killed Dee—if anyone had. Quite a party. To do this Miro must have woken this morning with one hell of a hangover. Joanna shrugged. Oh, the police would think of something. They always did.

The important thing was not to panic. Dee had shown the way out. "Where have you been?" she'd asked. "Did you stay at the flat?" Well, so she had. Everyone knew Jo had run from the party—so where had she gone? Where else but her flat?

She had passed a peaceful night there. Then come home to make up with Miro.

Joanna had rounded the house now, and was returning to the annex and the garages, untouched by fire. Where was the fire brigade? Never here when you needed them. Perhaps it was just as well. She stood still a moment and listened. Nothing. Pathetic. You'd think they'd put their foot down. But nowadays people wouldn't make the effort. Standards had slipped. She got into the Lexus, switched it on and edged gently round the house. Its back was untouched, the side seemed the same, but the front really did look quite dramatic. It was best she got away before the flames did attract attention.

The Lexus cruised down Miro's drive as if the car knew its own way. As she neared the tall iron gates they opened automatically to let Mrs. Vermont pass through. From now on, Joanna told herself, this was hers to command.